Ding Dong!
The Witch Is Dead

A Sebastian McCabe & Jeff Cody Mystery

ALSO BY DAN ANDRIACCO

The Sebastian McCabe & Jeff Cody Mysteries
No Police Like Holmes
Holmes Sweet Holmes
The 1895 Murder
The Disappearance of Mr. James Phillimore
Rogues Gallery
Bookmarked for Murder
Erin Go Bloody
Queen City Corpse
Death Masque
Too Many Clues
Murderers' Row
No Ghosts Need Apply
The English Garden Mystery
The Woman in Red
The Magician's Trunk

The Enoch Hale Trilogy (with Kieran McMullan)
The Amateur Executioner
The Poisoned Penman
The Egyptian Curse

Sherlock Holmes
Baker Street Beat
House of the Doomed
The Sword of Death

School for Sleuths
School for Sleuths
The Medium Is the Murder

Ding Dong!
The Witch Is Dead

A Sebastian McCabe & Jeff Cody Mystery

Dan Andriacco

Paperback ISBN 978-1-80424-751-8
ePub ISBN 978-1-80424-752-5
PDF ISBN 978-1-80424-753-2

Published by MX Publishing
335 Princess Park Manor, Royal Drive,
London, N11 3GX
www.mxpublishing.com
Cover design by

This one is for
Bob Sharfman
AKA the BF

CONTENTS

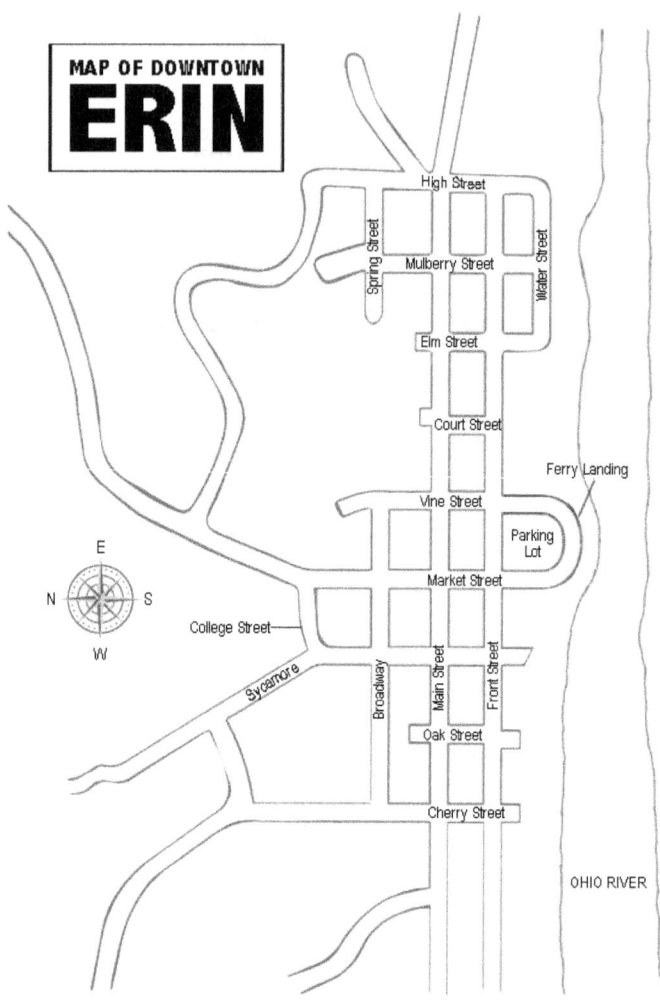

Chapter One
Murder by Moonlight

THE MURDER OF BETTY ERLANGER—by way of an arrow shot through her heart on the evening of Valentine's Day—would have been a natural to attract the unique crime-solving talents of Sebastian McCabe if ordinary police routine hadn't nabbed the archer so quickly. But then the case against the killer collapsed and Mac wound up in the thick of it. As usual.

Readers of the *Erin Observer & News-Ledger* opened their paper (or their app) on the morning of Friday, February 16, to read the huge headline **VALENTINE'S DAY MURDER** above the story, which began:

By **Johanna Rawls**

The body of 23-year-old Betty Erlanger, a teacher's aide at Gregory S. Meyer Elementary School, was found Thursday morning in Ramsey Park by a jogger. She had been shot in the heart with an arrow.

"The coroner's preliminary opinion is that she was likely killed the evening before," said Erin Police Chief Oscar Hummel. He declined to comment about the possible connection between the method of murder and the presumed date of death—Valentine's Day.

"That may be a factor, but it's too early to speculate," Hummel said. "We already have a person of interest, and we are making a very focused investigation."

"Is Oscar just blowing smoke with that 'person of interest' cliché?" Lynda asked, looking up from the newspaper with a quizzical expression on her lovely oval face as I was pouring cereal for the Cody kids. Although her business card says "Lynda Teal Cody—Storyteller" and she's written two family saga novels, my beloved spouse is still a journalist at heart. She drinks her coffee out of an old **YOUR SOURCE FOR LOCAL NEWS** mug from her *Observer* days. And she's turned several of Mac's cases into true-crime podcasts (much enhanced, in my opinion, by her throaty Lauren Bacall voice) for her former employer, the Grier media empire. Heck, our first date all those years ago was an interview.

"I don't think so," I responded. "I know he didn't call Mac for help on this one, because if he'd called Mac, Mac would have called me, and he didn't. That means that Oscar thinks he's got this, and maybe he has."

Even Mac professed to believe in the possibility.

"The fact that the murder circumstances are somewhat outré does not perforce mean that the solving of it requires my special insights," he told me on the phone later that day.

"Color me skeptical."

"And yet, Jefferson, I note that the day of the murder was not only the feast of St. Valentine but also Ash Wednesday, the beginning of Lent, a rare simultaneity."

"Meaning what?"

"Probably nothing. Still, one never knows."

Apparently, Mac had given up certitude for Lent.

Oscar didn't call that day, and the President's Day weekend was quiet at Chez Cody—or as quiet as possible with an 8-year-old and 6-year-old twins. (If you are not new to these chronicles, you've already met Donata, then in the second grade at St. Edward the Confessor School, and Sam and Jake, gearing up to ace first grade in the fall.)

FROM THE *OBSERVER* OF Tuesday, February 20:

EX-BOYFRIEND ARRESTED IN DEATH
*Witnesses say he threatened
Valentine's Day victim*

by Johanna Rawls

Troy Braggs, a 35-year-old auto mechanic, was arrested Monday on a charge of homicide in connection with the murder of Betty Erlanger, 23, who was slain by an arrow through her heart on Valentine's Day in Ramsey Park.

"Mr. Braggs was a former boyfriend of the victim who witnesses say was escorted off the playground of Gregory S. Meyer Elementary last week after threatening her and calling her a 'witch,'" said Erin Police Chief Oscar Hummel.

Hummel said Ms. Erlanger, a teacher's aide at the school, had recently broken up with Braggs and was now dating Artie Stone, 26, a waiter at the Erin Country Club.

"Ms. Erlanger received a Valentine's Day card purporting to be from Mr. Stone asking her to meet him at Ramsey Park 'in the moonlight' at 8 p.m.," Hummel said. "We believe the actual author of that card was Mr. Braggs, who used it to lure her to her place of death."

"That doesn't sound like Oscar," I told Aneliese Pokorny, my bottle-blonde office spouse (more formally, assistant director of marketing and communications at St. Benignus University) during our morning coffee klatch in my office. "There's no slang."

"He may have had a little help with the wording," Popcorn said, looking guilty.

I suspect she would like to make Oscar her spouse for real, except that won't happen as long as Oscar is living with his mother. Never mind that Popcorn and Oscar are both in their 60s. At any rate, each is the other's Significant Other.

The story went on to say:

Braggs belonged to a local archery club, the Straight Arrows, and was known to have a fiery temper, Hummel said. "He all but signed his name to the crime."

The accused has no verifiable alibi for the evening of the murder, claiming he was alone streaming the TV program "Forged in Fire," according to Hummel.

Bragg's attorney, Phoebe Farleigh, attacked the case against her client as purely circumstantial, adding . . .

"The Straight Arrows! It doesn't take a Sebastian McCabe to figure out where Oscar got that intel," I told Popcorn. "It must have been from Banfield by way of Gibbons. She's a member of the Straight Arrows."

"I'm not saying."

But Oscar's source was confirmed that Friday evening when Lynda and I found ourselves at Bobbie McGee's sports bar for fish and chips with Mac and my sister Kate, who is Mrs. McCabe. The McCabe offspring were babysitting their cousins. Among the other patrons of the popular establishment that evening were Lt. Col. L. Jack Gibbons, Oscar's laconic right-hand man as assistant chief, and Aurelia Banfield, whom Mac has referred to as Gibbons's inamorata. Banfield, assistant chief of the St. Benignus University Police, is five-foot-six of toned muscles, a one-legged Afghanistan vet with a better gym in her basement than the one I pay good money to belong to. Off-duty that night, she wore hoop earrings and had her brown hair in a ponytail.

"I didn't have to tell Jack that Troy's an archer, Seb," Banfield responded when Mac broached the subject after the usual round of hand pumping and hugs when we encountered each other. I don't know why she calls my corpulent, bearded, and formal-mannered brother-in-law by that casually shortened form of his first name; she's the only one who does. "Lord knows he's heard me complain about Troy often enough. That dude is bad news."

"Would you care to elaborate?" Mac pressed.

"Sure. Troy has the manners of a skunk and the temper of an alley cat, with sexual habits to match. And did I mention no self-discipline, which means he's super-immature? I tried to get him kicked out of the club because I was afraid that something would happen like what did happen. But the president of the club, Barry Lockland, is a good-old-boy friend of Troy's."

"You're lucky Braggs didn't set a target on you," Lynda told her.

"I can take care of myself."

Gibbons, who has been known to throw axes with Banfield on dates, almost grinned.

"Copy that," I said, using a favorite Banfield expression.

AGAINST ALL ODDS, MAC didn't get any closer to being involved in the murder by moonlight as the case moved toward trial in the coming months. Our good friend Johanna Rawls wrote an *Observer* profile of the Straight Arrows and a delicately crafted feature about how students at Gregory S. Meyer were reacting to the loss of their teacher's aide, Betty Erlanger. A catch-up story on the state of the case in March had Oscar and county prosecutor Marvin Slade noting that the brand of arrow used in the murder was the same one favored by Troy Braggs, with defense attorney Phoebe Farleigh countering by saying it was one of the most popular brands in America. I think that's known as pretrial maneuvering.

Then the case moved out of the headlines and off my radar for a while as life moved on that winter and into spring and summer for the Codys. Lynda's novel *Ink*, about four generations of a family-owned newspaper chain, garnered good reviews and she began thinking about another epic, but was too busy with the kids during summer break to get very far. I managed to spend my days in the office supervising Riley St. James (social media) and Sylvester Link (publications) instead of getting dragged away to help Mac help Oscar. Popcorn supervised me, of course.

We were a busy communication shop that summer, not putting out fires but telling our story. The contract of SBU's seventh president, Grant Kingsley ("GK"), was extended for another five years, giving Board of Trustees Chair Grace Langley the opportunity to say in my press release: "St. Benignus University is stronger than ever under President Kingsley's leadership and continues to grow both organically and by strategic acquisitions." In other words, he cut deadwood faculty and programs, bought up the failing but asset-rich Licking Falls University about an hour's drive from the SBU campus, and added popular new master's degree programs in health and leadership while keeping tuition increases moderate. Result: solid enrollment gains, outperforming our peers. We're approaching 1,700 undergrads and 300 graduate students in more than 25 majors.

While I was slaving away (except for a family vacation on Fripp Island), Sebastian McCabe launched a rereading of all the Nero Wolfe stories to celebrate the 90th anniversary of the first one, *Fer-de-Lance*, published in 1934. But you probably know that from watching his YouTube channel, "Mysteries with McCabe," on which he pontificated about the Wolfe stories as a mash-up of the traditional eccentric sleuth, represented by Wolfe, and the hard-boiled tradition seen in

Wolfe's assistant/irritant/narrator, Archie Goodwin. Maybe that combination is why Mac and I both like the Wolfe stories, the only literary taste we share.

In my world, the summer really ended on Monday, August 26, a week before Labor Day, with the beginning of Fall Semester. On Thursday of that week, I saw a photo of Troy Braggs, accompanied by his legal eagle Phoebe Farleigh, on page one of the *Erin Observer & News-Ledger* under the headline **MURDER TRIAL BEGINS TUESDAY**. It was a strange feeling to see a local headline involving the "M" word without having been an active participant in the unraveling of it. How did that make me feel? I didn't have much time to analyze it. Mac called me that afternoon.

"Friend Oscar has a small problem," he informed me.

"Define small."

"Troy Braggs has developed an alibi for the evening Betty Erlanger was killed."

"That's not a small problem."

"Oscar used more colorful language."

"I bet!"

"The prosecutor is not pleased."

Marvin Slade, he of the dyed-brown comb-over and the impeccable blue pinstriped suit, has been Sussex County prosecutor approximately forever. He's not Oscar's boss, but he tends to forget that. And he was campaigning for reelection that fall as a tough-on-crime prosecutor keeping us safe. His billboards and the few TV ads he had on the Cincinnati stations made it sound like the county would sink into a dystopian hellhole if Slade wasn't there to send all the bad guys to Devil's Island. To be fair, his assertion that his opponent, Legal Aid lawyer Glen Ritter, wanted to give small-time offenders a hug and an ice cream cone was only a slight exaggeration. The yard sign message "Stay Safe; Vote Slade" wasn't exactly inspiring but it got the idea across.

But now, with a high-interest, high-publicity trial underway, it looked like our veteran prosecutor might have trouble convicting a defendant who everybody in Erin thought was guilty. That wasn't a good re-election look.

"I suppose Oscar wants us to go and hold his hand."

"A little more than that, old boy."

I HAD SELDOM SEEN OSCAR Hummel's broad face under his balding dome look more dispirited. And that's saying a lot.

"Hell's bells!" he exploded within a few minutes after we took our accustomed seats in his police station office on Court Street. "That bastard Braggs—pardon my French—is guilty as hell."

The French word is actually bâtarde. Mac told me that once.

Oscar swung around to the Keurig machine behind him and sent a stream of caffeine-laced java pouring into the **I REFUSE TO ACT MY AGE** mug, which he then handed to Mac. I had some decaf myself, just to be sociable.

"What is the nature of Mr. Braggs's sudden alibi?" Mac asked after his first sip, because up to now Oscar hadn't gotten to the specifics.

"His former girlfriend, Robin Hauser. She says they were, you know, together for several hours that night."

Holy crap! The headline practically wrote itself: **HE WAS WITH ME, EX SAYS** or some such. Johanna's courthouse sources being impeccable, she was probably writing that story for the online version of the *Observer* as we spoke.

"Former girlfriend?" Mac repeated.

"Yeah, Braggs dumped this Hauser woman for Betty Erlanger. Apparently, he traded in for a younger model, Ms. Hauser being all of 29 compared to 23 for Ms. Erlanger."

"Uh-oh," I said. I got it right away, but it was Mac who put it into words as he said to Oscar:

"You have no doubt that she is lying in an attempt to regain the affections of the accused. However, you believe the jury will find her credible, assuming that a lover scorned would not be likely to commit perjury on behalf of the man who left her for another."

"That's it." Oscar chugged coffee.

"No doubt you are right, despite the fact that such an assumption would be erroneous for the simple reason that it is rational, and love has nothing to do with reason."

Oscar didn't directly respond to that. "Hauser has been visiting Braggs in jail. He's probably whispering sweet nothings and telling her he's innocent."

"Or even better," I offered, "spinning a fantasy about how Betty had some hold over him and the only way he could get rid of her so they could be together was with an arrow, even though nobody but her would understand the justice of that."

Pretty good, if I do say so myself!

"Whatever," Oscar said. "The important thing is that my crack troops had this thing all sewed up, now it's unsewed and Slade is breathing down my neck to—"

"No more metaphors and clichés, please!" Mac begged. "We understand the dilemma we are in." I noted the first-person plural pronoun—"we" were on the case. "We are morally certain that Troy Braggs is guilty of murder in the coldest blood. However, though there is a strong circumstantial case against him, it is not strong enough to overcome the alibi offered by Robin Hauser. Have you tried connecting Mr. Braggs to the greeting card luring Betty Erlanger to Ramsey Park?"

"Sure. That particular sickly-sweet Hallmark card was available at five different stores in Erin for weeks leading up to Valentine's Day. An average store clerk processes—what—dozens of transactions every day, even in a small town? If we'd gotten lucky, Braggs might have bought it from a clerk who remembered chatting because they were high school classmates or he worked on her car or some such, but we didn't get lucky."

"And in much the same way, the arrow used in the murder is a common brand, according to defense counsel," Mac mused.

"Right."

"Have you attempted to place Ms. Hauser some-where else on that evening in order to impeach the alibi she provided?"

Oscar nodded. "Holly"—that's the chief's executive assistant and spark plug, Holly Burdette—"scanned social media to find out who her friends are. Officers Bertsch, Mentzel, and Lehmann contacted all of them. Nobody ad-mitted being with her that night."

"What's with Mentzel, anyway?" I wondered. "I saw him the other day and he wasn't his normal cheerful self."

"Woman trouble. He got the old heave-ho a couple of months back and he's still not over it."

Staying focused on the slight matter of murder, Mac asked, "And you received no response to your appeals for anyone who saw anything in Ramsey Park that night to come forward?"

"If I had, I wouldn't have called you."

No other question was forthcoming as Mac stroked the graying hairs of his full-face beard.

"So, here we are," I summed up helpfully. *Here being up You-Know-Which Creek sans paddle.*

"This may take some time," Mac said.

"We haven't got any," Oscar pointed out. "The jurors have been chosen, and you may have noticed that the trial starts Tuesday."

I took that last comment as sarcasm, which is my superpower.

"We can but try," Mac said. "The motto of the firm."[1]

We were barely on the sidewalk outside the police station before Mac fired up one of his hand-rolled Antonio de la Cova cigars, each of which costs five times as much as a box of healthful cereal. (And have you seen the price of cereal lately?) He claims that helps him think, never mind that nicotine is a poison once used in a mystery novel by Mac himself.

"Well, genius?" I prodded, after letting him take a few unhealthful puffs.

"Blast it, Jefferson, I am not a trained elephant!"

No comment.

THE FERTILE BRAIN OF Sebastian McCabe remained free of storms that morning and into the afternoon. But about the time of day that I look forward to home and hearth, he gave me a call. Sometimes I miss the old days of distinctive ring

---

[1] Quoting Sherlock Holmes in "The Adventure of the Creeping Man."—
S.McC.

tones, which are now passé; Mac's tune on my phone was "You're So Vain," which always put me in a good mood.

"We may have what I believe you would characterize as a 'break' in the Erlanger case," he announced before I even had a chance to answer with something snappy like, "Cody's Fun House, chief funster speaking."

"What kind of break?"

"An eyewitness to the murder. I am at Witch's Brew, with which you are well acquainted. Meet me here as soon as you can."

Chapter Two
It Takes a Witch

I WAS ALL TOO WELL "acquainted" with the "metaphysical supply shop" called Mistress Quant's Witch's Brew from that magician's trunk business the previous year.[2] The crystal skulls and dragons in the window of the store add a certain eldritch atmosphere to an otherwise staid part of Mulberry Street, just a block from the Public Library of Erin and Sussex County and Bruce Gordon's floral emporium. If you were looking for charms, incense, body oils, tarot readings, and/or Wiccan and pagan ritual items, that was your go-to store in Erin. And have I mentioned that the proprietor was a witch? That isn't name-calling; she was a practitioner of Wicca.

I have to admit I got a bit of the creepy-crawlies when I entered the place. I'd never been inside, having encountered owner Zoraida Quant in other venues. Even if I hadn't, I would have recognized her curly gray hair and blue glasses from the campaign posters for her unsuccessful city council campaign. After finishing 22nd in a field of 22 for eight spots, she'd made a second career out of her Instagram channel lambasting local community figures, probably getting more traffic than "Mysteries with McCabe" over on YouTube.

---

[2] See *The Magician's Trunk* (MX Publishing, 2024).

That I knew, not from having watched any of the short videos, but from a feature story in the *Observer* by Hadley Reams, who also covers SBU and education in general.

As I walked in, Quant was standing next to Mac, quite a bit shorter than his five-ten, wearing a loose dress with short sleeves that showed off her pentagram tattoo. I caught the tail end of a sentence: ". . . a wolf's head?"

"No, madam; that is a hound, and not of the Baskervillian variety." He was referring to the head of his walking stick. "Ah, Jefferson! Thank you for coming. Ms. Quant asked me here to impart information of vital importance in person." He turned to her. "Would you please repeat that for my friend?"

"Why?"

Because if you're making it up you might not get the invented details straight the second time.

From long experience, I know how the mind of Sebastian McCabe works. But he merely said:

"I would like to hear it again."

Quant sighed, as if this was heavy lifting, but I had the impression she was putting it on a bit. She probably enjoyed the attention. "On February 14, I was collecting hellebore in Ramsey Park by moonlight."

"Hellebore!" That sounded hellish to me.

"The hellebore flower is also called a Lenten rose, and it blooms in February," Mac informed me.

"It has all kinds of magical uses," Quant said, then went on to specify: "Love spells, divination, exorcism, purification rituals, warding off negative energies."

Very useful—like duct tape.

"Anyway, that's when I saw that guy shoot the young woman with an arrow."

Well, I knew this was coming—Mac had said "eyewitness"—but it was still a bit of a rush.

"I saw her first—that Betty Erlanger, although I didn't know her name at the time. She walked into the park and kind of stood there near the swing set, looking around. Then Braggs stepped out from behind a tree with a bow and arrow in his hand. That's who it was, Troy Braggs. I saw his picture in the paper when the trial started. He said—talking to Ms. Erlanger, you understand—'Nobody ditches me.' Then he shot her with an arrow in the heart and took off. She was already dead when I got to the body."

"And you didn't report it?" I said, utterly astonished.

"There was nothing I could do, and I knew the body would be found by somebody else, probably in the morning, but that would be soon enough."

"But you saw the killer!"

"I don't like to make a splash"—*since when?*—"and I thought I could stay out of this because the killer was under arrest within a few days."

Mac raised an eyebrow. "That is hardly credible. I find it much more likely that you did not make a report because you were taking the hellebores to which you had no right. The technical name for that is theft, although the idea that the police or prosecutor would be interested in such a minor infraction strains credibility."

The witch shrugged.

"Why have you come forward now?"

"I didn't want to, but the cops and Slade are blowing it. I saw online today that some ex-girlfriend gave that killer a phony alibi and they haven't been able to get her to tell the truth. That's one reason I'm getting involved. Plus, I read a while back that Braggs called Betty Erlanger a witch, as if that were a bad thing. He deserves to go down, and it looks like I have to help make that happen."

"Why didn't you go to Oscar Hummel or the prosecutor with your story, given that you'll have to talk to both of them anyway?" I wanted to know.

She snorted. "Those fools? Why should I let them get the credit, which would happen if I did this quietly? I'd rather have you take me to them as their new key witness and let it be reported that way in the paper. And I'll play you up, not them, on Instagram."

"Do you have a lot of followers?" I wondered. About this time, Taylor Swift had a reported 283 million followers on Instagram, 95 million on X, 80 million on Facebook, 57 million on YouTube, and 25 million on TikTok.

"Almost 5,000 so far," Quant said. "Not getting rich from it, but not bad for a Podunk town like this." She turned to Mac. "Have you seen my channel?"

"I have not yet had that pleasure."

"You should." She changed topics. "I kind of like you, McCabe. You're full of yourself, and you talk like a dictionary, but you figure it out in the end. If I were murdered, I'd want you on the case."

Talk about a mixed compliment!

"Tell you what," she went on, "I'll give you a free tarot reading. I normally charge twenty-five bucks."

"That is very generous of you. However, my faith as a Catholic . . ."

"It's just for fun," I interrupted, curious to see how this would go.

By this time Quant had already sat at a round table, which I deduced she used for the tarot readings. According to the sign on her window, she offered such by appointment. With a shrug, Mac sat down opposite her.

"As you wish, Mistress Quant," he said. "I suppose it could do no harm, given my mental reservation."

The witch shuffled the deck and pulled out a card. It was an image of a skeleton in black armor on a white horse. The skeleton carried a flag with the Roman numeral XIII— 13. And just to make the symbolism clear, the word DEATH appeared at the bottom of the card.

"Uh-oh," I said.

Chapter Three
The Wheels of Justice

"IT MAY NOT MEAN a literal death," I explained to Lynda that evening at the Cody bungalow after the kids were down for the night. She was bent over her toes, honey-blonde curls dangling fetchingly over her well-filled-out red kimono as she painted her nails pink and green to look like Labor Day picnic watermelons. It was the first chance I'd had to debrief her, although I was finding it a little hard to concentrate.

"I certainly hope not, darling," she responded. "Life would be a lot duller without Sebastian McCabe around."

"For sure! But according to our local witch, the death card could just mean a major transformation in the life of the person who's dealt it."

"Still, the *death* card!" Lynda gave a theatrical shiver as she closed up the bottle of nail polish. Her husky voice added a certain frisson to the statement. "How did Mac react?"

"Oh, you know, with a bunch of big words that mean 'what a crock.' I expect somewhat shorter words from Slade when he finds out we have an eyewitness to murder but she's a witch."

"A WITCH! WHAT ARE YOU smoking, McCabe?"

"Nothing hallucinatory, I assure you, Mr. Slade."

"She says 'witch,' but you can call her a Wiccan if that sounds better," I put in.

Mac had called the prosecutor's private cell number on Friday morning and put him on the speakerphone, knowing that I would enjoy this.

"I find Ms. Quant's testimony highly credible," Mac added. He went on to give an almost verbatim account of our encounter with Quant, leaving out the part where she called Oscar and Slade fools.

"She is eager to share all this with you, but insists that I accompany her to your office," Mac concluded. Quant had also more than hinted that media would be welcome to record the handover. But Mac knew that "bridge too far" (as he expressed it to me) would ring a death knell on his reasonably cooperative relationship with the prosecutor.

"Fine," Slade huffed. "Bring her in as soon as you can, but then you're gone. You can't sit in while I question her. She can, of course, bring counsel if she wishes."

She didn't wish.

We found out later what happened:

"Slade asked her all kinds of questions to try to make sure she was really there during the murder: What was the weather like that night? Was there a full moon? There wasn't, by the way; it was a waxing crescent. What was Troy wearing? What was Betty wearing? She nailed it all."

This was conveyed to me on Tuesday evening, the day after Labor Day and the day the trial started, by Lynda's BFF, Sister Mary Margaret Malone, also known as Sister Polly. Triple M (as I call her) had stopped by to pick up Lynda for a meeting of the Captain Nemo Society, the science-fiction book club that gathers monthly at Mo's Mysteries and

Marvels bookstore. The good sister is a sci-fi fan; Lynda just likes to socialize with people over the age of eight.

"And you know this how?" I asked.

"Louise has good ears, and she knew you'd be interested. Don't tell anybody but Mac."

Louise LaRosa works at the prosecutor's office and is also a member of the aforementioned group of readers, along with Holly Burdette and young attorney Sally Fair. If things had worked out differently, I wouldn't be sharing that conversation.

BUT I'M GETTING AHEAD of the story by talking about Tuesday. Greasing the wheels of justice, Slade announced his new witness to the press over the Labor Day weekend, even though she wouldn't be taking the stand until the end of his case—the final and most damning evidence. The prosecutor was determined to set all the groundwork for an airtight case and then bring in Quant as the finishing stroke. But, playing a media game with an eye on the election, he also wanted maximum exposure for his witness in advance. And he got it.

I knew what was coming when Mac related to me his *Observer* interview with Johanna Rawls after Slade made the big reveal about Quant on Saturday afternoon. The interchange went something like this:

JOHANNA: "Hi, Mac. My source tells me that you brought the witness in the Erlanger murder case to the prosecutor's office."

MAC: "You have good sources, Johanna."

(Quant herself or LaRosa? I could flip a coin.)

JOHANNA: "How did that come about?"

MAC: "I prefer not to say."

JOHANNA: "You haven't been involved in this case up to now, have you?"

MAC: "I have not."

JOHANNA: "So what changed?"

MAC: "I do not think that is relevant to the trial now underway."

JOHANNA: "Maybe not, but it would be interesting. All right, never mind. Phoebe Farleigh, the defense attorney, has called into question the reliability of the witness, Zoraida Quant, because she claims to be a witch. How do you react to that?"

MAC: "I do not."

JOHANNA: "Come on, Mac, throw me a bone here, will you?"

MAC: "My acquaintance with Ms. Quant is a peripheral one and not relevant. I can say only that I am quite certain the prosecutor has thoroughly vetted her testimony and accurately assessed its reliability."

None of that appeared in Monday's *Observer* story, **MURDER WITNESS EMERGES**, with the subhead, *Owner of occult shop says she saw slaying.* In a model of journalistic self-restraint, Johanna didn't use the word "witch" until the fourth paragraph: "Quant, who has described herself as a witch . . ." The only quote from her was, "I'm saving my testimony for court, but be sure to check me out on Instagram." Farleigh and Slade each had their say—"unreliable witness" vs. "checks out on every verifiable fact about the murder night." The Associated Press, Central News Service, and the Cincinnati TV stations played the witch angle with a heavier hand, despite Slade's best efforts to put the focus on the upcoming testimony rather than the testifier.

"Johanna is such a good reporter," I opined, looking up from the newspaper and my cereal that morning.

"And don't I know it!" Lynda agreed.

As news editor of the *Observer* in earlier days, Lynda had been Johanna's mentor. The two remain close.

"Then why is she working for a small-town newspaper instead of *The Daily Planet?*" I wondered.

Lynda bit her lip in thought. "Other than the fact that the *Planet* doesn't exist outside of DC comics and movies, I suppose it's because she'd either have to move or have a long daily commute. Even Cincinnati is almost an hour away. And she may have sort of told me she doesn't want to leave town because of Seth, who wouldn't want to live far from his family. They don't exactly travel much."

Seth Miller's parents and siblings are Amish, of which there are a lot in our part of Ohio. The Amish do travel, even long distances, but not easily. Tall Rawls and less-than-tall Seth, an easygoing dental hygienist, had been an item for years by that fall.[3] Apparently one of them was slow to commit, and I didn't think it was Johanna.

"I ought to give that boy a talking-to about taking the plunge," I told Lynda.

"Yeah, you ought to. And if he balks, tell him I said he's an idiot."

---

[3] See *Erin Go Bloody* (MX Publishing, 2016).

Chapter Four

Crime on Court Street

EVEN THOUGH I HAD trail mix and an apple packed for lunch that day, I had the notion of calling Seth around 1:15 to see if he was free for lunch. I figured—correctly—that a dental hygienist working downtown would have appointments at noon but might be free shortly thereafter. What I didn't foresee was the reception my call would get.

"Wow, I can't believe you're calling, Jeff! How did you know I need you and Professor McCabe?"

McCabe? Hey, I've got this, Seth! I'm not sure Mac is the man to go to for romantic advice.

"Call me psychic and let's do lunch."

Daniel's Apothecary was an easy choice. On Main Street facing the law offices of Farleigh & Farleigh, the drug store was just around the corner from Dr. Marcum's Court Street dental office where Seth works. It's been owned and operated by the Daniel family since 1904, but the décor of the soda shop part, operated by Jacqui Daniel, is fixed at about 1959. There you'll find a jukebox, fountain drinks, black and chrome tables, and red and white stools at the long counter. Seth and I sat at a table under a Route 66 clock and a Marilyn Monroe poster.

"About Johanna," I began after we placed our orders with a cheery, round server named Vern. Mine was an Elvis, which is a peanut butter and sliced banana sandwich on grilled Texas toast. Vern warned me that the peanut butter contains peanuts in case I was allergic. She does that every time.

Seth—dark-haired, bespectacled, five-foot-six, and in his mid-thirties like Johanna—looked like I'd just told him I don't floss my teeth, both shocked and puzzled. "Johanna?" he said before I could get any further. "What does she have to do with this?"

"Everything, I hope! She's a wonderful person and —that is, I mean—" I backed up. "What do you think we're here to talk about?"

"The robbery." He looked at me like he thought I was a dullard, and I was in no mood to disagree.

"What robbery?"

"My bike. Somebody stole my bike this morning. I thought you'd bring Professor McCabe to find the thief and get it back."

"He's busy." *Probably playing his bagpipes.* I tried to re-orient to what was apparently the subject at hand. "Don't you have one of those fancy-schmancy e-bikes?"

"I wouldn't call it that. It's a Turbo Vado SL 4.0 Step-Through, which cost me just under four thousand dollars three years ago. "

I almost spilled my Caffeine-Free Diet Coke. *Four thousand dollars for a bike!* That's a long way from the cost of my ancient Schwinn when it was new.

"It was cheaper than a decent used car at the time because the COVID car scarcity was already on. But I don't drive anyway, so I don't know why I said that." Seth was babbling, probably the strain of being a crime victim. "There are more expensive and more powerful e-bikes, and ones that are better on hills, but the Turbo Vado SL suits my needs."

"Okay, let's take this from the top," I said. "What happened?"

Seth told me that he bikes to work, as I do most days. In case of really bad rain or snow, he hitches a ride from Johanna. (They don't cohabit, as Mac would say, not that it's any of your business.) He parks the bike at a stand just a few doors south of his office, which is near the intersection of Front Street. In addition to the dentist's office, Court Street is home to the Auld Lang Syne antique store, Long John Gold's Treasure Chest pawnshop, a half dozen or more law offices, the police station, and the Sussex County Court House on the corner of Court and Main. (See the map of downtown Erin on page 10.)

"This morning around eleven I had fifteen minutes between appointments, so I went out to get a cup of coffee at Beans & Books—I love their Guatemalan blend—and I noticed that the bike rack where I always park was empty. Somebody stole my Turbo Vado!"

"Did you make a police report?"

"I haven't had time. The patients come first."

As one of his patients, I couldn't argue with that.

"Besides," Seth added, "I thought maybe you and Mac could handle it. You know, maybe the thief is somebody who needs the bike more than I do and I don't want to get him into trouble."

That was pure Seth.

I later found out that by one count about 2 million bikes are stolen every year in America, worth a total of about $1 billion. As a result, thousands of amateurs around the country make it a hobby to find and return stolen bikes, which is kind of cool. But I didn't know this on that September morning. All I knew was that a friend needed help.

"Well, you should make a police report anyway," I said. "You don't have to file charges if you decide that mercy should triumph over justice." *Where did that come from?* "You want the police to be on the lookout for your bike in case the thief was a joyrider who left it somewhere. Not likely, but it could happen."

Then I put on my metaphorical deerstalker and started asking questions like Sebastian McCabe or L. Jack Gibbons. "Didn't you have a lock on the bike?"

"Sure! In fact—this is kind of embarrassing—it kept me from using the bike myself a few days ago."

"How so?"

"I came out of the gym, Nouveau Shape, and found that the key wasn't in my pocket. I had to get a ride home from a gym friend to get my other key."

Fascinating, but time to shift gears.

"How fast can your bike go?"

"With motorized assist, up to 28 miles an hour."

"The thief could get pretty far from downtown in a short time," I noted. "This isn't exactly a metropolis. He or she may have the bike posted on Facebook Marketplace for sale by now."

"I hadn't thought of that."

That's why I'm the detective.

"Let's check that out," I said.

Which we did, on my cell. But Seth's bike wasn't posted on Facebook Marketplace, that day or ever.

"I'll talk to Mac and see if he has any ideas," I finally said, reluctantly.

By the time we finished our meals and talked through the stolen bike business, Seth had to get back to the dental office. So, I didn't get a chance to tell him that Lynda said he was an idiot for slow-walking the Rawls-Miller relationship. I couldn't in good conscience hit Seth with that and then send him back to the office to work on some victim's teeth. In fact, we never did have that discussion. We didn't need to.

"SOMEBODY STOLE SETH MILLER'S e-bike, and he needs our help to get it back," I told Mac later that afternoon. I gave him all the details just as I've given them to you, even the part about Seth's misadventures with his bike lock.

Mac raised an eyebrow. I couldn't see that because we were talking on our cells, but I know him. He raised an eyebrow. Maybe two.

"Good heavens, Jefferson! Are we degenerating into an agency for recovering lost lead pencils?"

"Eh?" The allusion to pencils was lost on me.[4]

"Surely this is a matter for what Holmes called 'the official force' with their capacity to be on the alert for the stolen object."

"Well, if you don't have the imagination . . ."

I let that jab at the McCabe ego trail off.

"Hmmm," he mused. "It is not inconceivable that there could be something more interesting here. Suppose, for example, that the bicycle was not the ultimate object of the theft but ancillary to it."

"As in?"

---

[4] I was quoting Sherlock Holmes from the opening scene of "The Adventure of the Copper Beeches."—*S. McC.*

"Imagine, for example, that our young friend had a saddlebag on his bicycle and a thief hid some stolen object there on the spur of the moment—rather like the Countess of Morcar's blue carbuncle hidden in the crop of a goose—because the thief knew he would be searched. And when it came time to retrieve the object, he or she realized it would look suspicious to remove it from a saddlebag and walk away. So the thief rode away on the stolen bicycle instead."

"That's a lot of imagining."

"I do not find that a valid criticism."

"And don't forget that there was a lock on the bike, which would have discouraged a spur-of-the-moment theft."

"A valid point, I must concede."

When I caught Seth later between patients, he informed me that, "Gosh, yeah, I have a saddlebag. It had my lunch in it. Thanks again for picking up the tab at Daniel's."

That was an added fact, but not particularly helpful so far as I could see.

Seth said he'd reported the bike theft to the police, so I gave Oscar a call to nudge him a bit.

"We'll keep our eagle eyes out for it downtown while we canvass for witnesses to the robbery this morning," he assured me.

"What robbery?"

"Long John Gold's Treasure Chest, the pawnshop."

"I know the interest rate Long John charges on loans is sky-high, but to call it robbery—"

"Some dude in long blond hair and a beard—probably a disguise—walked in and waved a gun at Long John, demanding that he empty the till." Long John's real name is

Harvey Gold and he lives with his ex-wife, who's a family counselor. It's complicated.

"That's almost directly across the street from you!" I told Oscar, although he knew that.

"Yeah, well, we don't spend a lot of time looking out our windows. The robber got away with over six hundred dollars in cash on hand. Don't tell Mac. We got this one, no upmarket theories needed."

I told Mac, of course. He was delighted.

"While coincidence of timing and location can never be ruled out in real life, it is highly likely that Seth Miller's bicycle thief was escaping from the scene of the crime at Long John's—a notably short distance away—on a stolen vehicle. As an electric bicycle it had speed while at the same time being nimbler in traffic than an automobile. My tentatively offered saddlebag theory thus comes a cropper, Jefferson, although I will note that Seth's saddlebag was a handy place to put the stolen cash."

"Well, that's that, then. It's a plain vanilla robbery and nothing more to be done except find the stolen bike."

"Not quite, old boy. Can you not see the implication?"

When I confessed that I did not, he rolled out the new and improved McCabe Stolen E-Bike Theory for me. And when Seth Miller—to his intense surprise—received a text message late that afternoon from a burner phone telling him he could find his bike on the riverfront bike trail, Mac knew that this time he was right.

ON TUESDAY, SEPTEMBER 3, the trial of Troy Braggs began with opening arguments and routine matters, no fireworks. But I wasn't there. In my day job, I was heavily involved in the free speech controversy that was rocking the Ivy Leagues and filtering down even to our little corner of academia. It was a hot button that kept being pressed in different ways, starting the previous year and continuing into 2024 in a context of international turmoil that I don't need to get into here. I'm sure you remember. I managed to snag an interview with GK about the topic on National Public Radio, of which our campus station WIJC is an affiliate. On this matter, our university president spoke from his heart and needed virtually no help from his ace communication guru (yours truly).

"A university is about free inquiry, or it is about nothing at all," he told iconic NPR interviewer Carl Lomax. "It is essential that students feel free to challenge their classmates, their professors, and even settled narratives. You can't have true freedom without the freedom to challenge, which includes the freedom to be wrong.

"When I was a student, I frequently argued with my professors; they let me do so and they didn't penalize my grades. Looking back, I might have actually been wrong once or twice, but I learned from the dialogue." GK didn't mention this was at the Air Force Academy, where he later taught as a colonel before launching a civilian career that eventually put him in the C-suite at the Altiora Corp. He came to SBU as president after a stint as chair of the board of trustees.

"Of course, that freedom of speech applies to everybody, which means that there is no right to shout down a guest speaker or another student."

"Have you had protest rallies at your small Catholic institution?"

"Yes—small ones. They've been peaceful and orderly, in line with our very clear policies. I might mention that although we are a Catholic university, we have students who are Protestants, Jews, and Muslims. All are welcome here, and all are safe from violence and discrimination, but they are not safe from hearing ideas they may disagree with."

Not only did that sound good; he also meant it.

I'd just returned to my office, with a good feeling about the interview, when Mac showed up.

"Do you have time to join me in a visit to Mr. Gold's establishment?"

"Of course not. I'm a highly paid professional."

I could hear Popcorn laugh across the hallway.

WE'D BEEN TO LONG John Gold's Treasure Chest before on business—ours, not Long John's. True to his name, he stands about six-seven, half a foot taller than yours truly, and weighs maybe 250 pounds after a heart-attack-induced weight loss. His crew-cut hair, mustache, and small beard were all dishwater gray, not unexpected in a man with his 70th birthday in the rearview mirror. Tattoos of mermaids on his arms and a gold earring in one ear completed the carefully cultivated piratical image.

"Hello, gentlemen!" he coughed out in an asthmatic wheeze. "Welcome to Long John Gold's Treasure Chest, where somebody else's misfortune is your good fortune."

With the last word, a look of recognition came into his eyes. "McCabe and Cody! You must be here about the robbery."

Mac nodded. "Indeed, sir! I take it that you have no strong notion as to who the robber could be?"

"If I did, I would have told that cop, Bertsch. She's a cute one."

You should tell her that. I'd love to see the look on her cute face before she flipped you.

While I was musing, Gold went on:

"He was wearing a disguise that wouldn't have fooled my six-year-old granddaughter—a cheap wig and beard of the kind they sell at Walmart or Target for Halloween."

"Didn't you think that a little odd?" I asked.

"Odd? Are you kidding? Weirdos come in here all the time. As long as they're good customers, I don't judge. But then he pulled out a Glock, told me to turn over my cash, and ordered me to get on the floor while he escaped. I say 'he' not because of the fake beard but because I could tell from the build and the way he walked that it was a man."

I was impressed.

"There were no other customers in the store?" Mac asked.

"There usually aren't at that time of day. Why are you guys here, anyway? This kind of non-lethal crime doesn't seem to be up your alley. It only rated a few paragraphs in the *Observer* this morning: 'Pawnshop Near Police Station Robbed.' At least they had the name and address of the store right. There's no such thing as bad publicity."

Oh, yes there is. I've had to deal with plenty of it in my day job.

"We are here because the owner of the stolen getaway vehicle is a friend of ours," Mac explained. *Besides, we're between murders at the moment, except for that Valentine's Day business.* "That is to say, our friend Seth Miller is how we became involved. I remain intrigued even though his bicycle has been recovered."

"Intrigued by what?"

"Mr. Gold, the fact that the robber most likely knew the time of day when you would be the least busy confirmed for me what I had already suspected: The culprit is either one of your customers or someone who frequents this street—or perhaps both. Escape by e-bicycle was almost certainly not a spur-of-the-moment decision. Ergo, the fleeing felon had to know that the vehicle would be available, knowledge that would be had by someone who is often nearby or patronizes your enterprise. Odds on the latter are especially strong. Most likely you sold him the gun he pointed at you." This last was true, given that guns were a big part of the Treasure Chest's business, but also a way to get Long John's cooperation.

What Mac wasn't telling the pawnbroker was that the thief must have also been a friend or at least a friendly acquaintance of Seth Miller in order to (a) know that the bike was his, (b) somehow get the key to his bike lock, (c) have Seth's phone number to call and tell him where his e-bike was, and (d) want to do so. I'm sure I would have figured that out eventually if Mac hadn't told me.

"Would you be willing to share with us a list of customers whose physical dimensions are compatible with those of the thief?" Mac asked.

"To nail that scumbag? Damn right."

"That list need not be comprehensive. Your newest customers will do nicely. My premise is that someone only recently came into a desperate need of funds, began by pawning some items for cash, and realized that there was more cash to be had in this establishment."

Here's the list of names Long John gave Mac in writing, and what he knew about each:

Pete Gregory—"retired and very fond of beer";

Lenny Swann—"clerk at Auld Lang Syne antique store down the street";

Luke Parks—"does something at Altiora";

Bob Kenner—"works at Lawrence's IGA, apparently not a very good poker player."

BEFORE MAC SHOWED THE names to Seth just a few minutes later in Dr. Marcum's office, he made a production number out of it. After first explaining his certainty that the bike thief was also the pawnshop robber, he said:

"I predict that one of the individuals on this list of recent customers of Mr. Gold is also the 'gym friend' who gave you a ride when you lost the key to your bicycle lock."

Seth's eyes widened behind his glasses as he looked at the list.

"Lenny Swann! How did you know?"

"Whoever stole your bicycle had a key to the lock. How did the miscreant get that key? By stealing your original one and duplicating it. When did you notice the key missing? After your workout at the gymnasium—where a fellow fitness enthusiast that you regarded as a casual friend would have access to it in the locker room. Mr. Swann also works on Court Street, where he would see your electric and therefore quite speedy bicycle parked there every day. That no doubt sparked his scheme to use it for his escape."

"I'm sure you're right. Lenny asked me one day to show him how the bike worked. Wow, you are awesome, Mac!"

Mac probably agreed but didn't say so. Instead, he asked whether Seth could go with us to pay Lenny Swann a visit. Seth begged off, saying he was working until 6 P.M. But I think he didn't have the heart for the confrontation.

So, Mac and I walked down the street without him. Chitchatting along the way, we agreed that Phoebe Farleigh's attempts to undercut Zoraida Quant as a witness were unlikely to save Troy Braggs from going down for the Betty Erlanger murder. Farleigh was relatively new to criminal law, and I admired her for taking on some tough cases even as I was glad that justice was served.

Auld Lang Syne had that musty antique store smell that makes me want to sneeze. Even worse than that, some of the antiques were toys I remembered from my childhood.

Lenny Swann, the only clerk present although not the owner, was in his fifties, balding, wearing a Hawaiian shirt. We recognized him from Seth's description.

"Good afternoon," he greeted us. "Feel free to look around."

"We have just come from Long John Gold's Treasure Chest and Seth Miller, in that order," Mac informed him. "You robbed both of them."

"Oh shit!"

Swann crumpled faster than a politician's campaign promise, babbling a mishmash of confession and excuse in one rush. What Mac had described to Long John as "a desperate need for funds" had come about because Swann had lost several thousand dollars to an internet scammer. Even worse, he was afraid to tell his wife, who had very strong opinions about his money management skills. I thought maybe he needed to see Long John's wife, the family relationship counselor, although I didn't say so.

"WHAT NOW?" I ASKED Mac back on the sidewalk.

"We must inform Oscar, of course. It will be up to the victims whether they wish to press charges."

In case you're wondering, neither did. That surprised me in the case of Long John. When I asked him about it some weeks later, he growled something about the need for "second chances." That brought him up a notch in my estimation, although I had the impression he was talking from personal experience.

"You do realize that if this were fiction, the villain would have been somebody we'd already met in the story," I told Mac.

"*If*, old boy."

He had me there.

"No doubt your readers, should you ever write about this small endeavor, will be disappointed on that score," he acknowledged. "I am not, however. After all, it is an even greater achievement to reveal the thief to be someone we never knew existed until a short while ago."

I thought he was just gassing, and maybe he was. But Mac would hearken back to the solution of this minor case in a strange way when he solved the two murders that were soon to occur.

WHAT WITH ALL THAT talking over the crimes of Lenny Swann, and yakking more about the Braggs trial, we were back on campus and at my office before I knew it. This was a relatively rare appearance for the big guy in the impressive old Georgian-style structure known as the Gamble Building; he usually talks to me on the phone or summons me across campus to his office in Herbert Hall.

Just as we arrived and exchanged greetings with Popcorn, his cell rang.

"Ah, it is Rebecca," he announced, already walking back toward the hallway. "I must take this."

In private, he meant. Father-daughter stuff, I presumed.

I was giving Popcorn a dramatic account of our afternoon, which of course enthralled her ("No way!"), when Mac wandered back in with a dazed look on his hirsute face. Even his signature bowtie, this one blue with yellow stripes, somehow looked dispirited. Popcorn had a cup of coffee in his hand before he sat down. Then she sat down, too.

"You look like somebody sucker punched you," I said.

"Colorfully put, but quite accurate."

"I'm a writer. What happened?"

"Rebecca is moving to New York!"

The oldest McCabe offspring, who had turned 25 that summer, was a graduate of SBU in graphic design. For some years she'd been living in the comfortable apartment above Mac's garage that had been my own home in bachelor days.

"For a job?" I asked.

"Yes. At Hathaway & Cole, the fashion house."

I knew that name! I'd seen their ads in the super-glitzy *WSJ* magazine, which comes into our house with the *Wall Street Journal* once a month. Said ads feature such bargains as a thousand bucks for a purse just because it has the H&C logo on the outside. That's a little much for me. I might be willing to go north of $75 for a purse that I judge Lynda-worthy.

"Wow!" Popcorn said.

"It sounds like a great opportunity," I put in. *Some of all that money H&C is taking in must be going to the talent.*

I didn't mention the elephant in the room, and I don't mean Mac. My niece had been struggling ever since finding a dead body,[5] and maybe she needed to get away from people and places that reminded her of that.

"Although Amanda"—the younger McCabe daughter and middle child, a Ph.D/M.D. student at the University of Cincinnati—"no longer lives at home, she is not far away and returns frequently," Mac said. "New York is an entirely different matter!"

I could see that it would be no use reminding him that he visited New York at least once a year, for Baker Street Irregulars Weekend each January, and was intimately familiar with mid-town Manhattan. He was clearly gutted.

"Maybe you need an empty-nester coach," Popcorn said.

"Is that really a thing?" I asked.

"Would I make that up? Could I? I'm no fictioneer. Certified coaches can get paid two hundred and fifty bucks an hour."

"Not by me, they wouldn't! And anyway, Mac and Kate aren't really empty-nesters—Brian still lives at home." My nephew was 20 and a theater major at SBU.

Mac remained glumly silent.

"I read about a guy who paid two thousand dollars for weekly video conferences with a coach after seeing videos served up by TikTok's algorithm," Popcorn informed us. "And this was when his second son went off to college, even though he still had a daughter in high school."

---

[5] See *The Woman in Red* (MX Publishing, 2023).

Dumbfounded, I had no response to that.

"I suppose that Kate and I will adapt to the change in time," Mac said gloomily.

That's when it clicked.

"Change!" I repeated. "This is a major life change for you. As in, transformation. Almost like a death of sorts."

Popcorn, fully informed about our encounter with Zoraida Quant, got it right away. "This could be what that death card was all about!" she told Mac.

"Nonsense!"

"But you do believe in the supernatural," she pressed, seemingly enthralled.

"Indeed, I do, Ms. Pokorny, and precognition as well. Tarot cards are another matter entirely. They can be read to mean almost anything, and convincingly so by one talented in cold readings." By that I knew he meant the techniques that mentalists, psychics, fortune-tellers, and mediums use to make high-probability guesses about clients or audience members. Mac was a dab hand at that himself, dating back to his youthful days as a street magician in Europe.

"I still think I should tell Zoraida Quant about this," I said.

But I never had a chance.

On Wednesday morning, the second day of the trial in which the witch was scheduled to testify against Troy Braggs—a day the *Observer*'s front page was dominated by veteran journalist Bernard J. Silverstein's account of the opening arguments of said trial—she was found bludgeoned to death in her shop.

Chapter Five

The Witch Is Dead

OSCAR CALLED MAC TO the scene around 9:30 that morning "because it's weird, and you specialize in weird. And also, you were chummy with the deceased."

"Hardly that, Oscar!" Mac protested. Or so he related to me on the way there, having snatched me away from my office as he is wont to do.

In daylight—and this is the first time I'd paid much attention to it in daylight—Mistress Quant's Witch's Brew and environs weren't so creepy. In fact, that end of town had been perking up of late. Mulberry intersects with Front Street, and the newly energized Gatsby's Gastropub is at High and Front Streets, not far from the upscale Harridan Hotel. Forgive me for my passing thought that Quant's landlord could probably do better than a "metaphysical supply shop" and tarot reader in that building. But I digress.

Don't tell anybody that McCabe & Cody slipped through the crime scene tape, as is our habit, being careful not to touch anything.

"We can rule out the obvious," I assured Oscar. "Troy Braggs didn't do it because he was in your jail, no matter when it happened."

Oscar gave me a sour look, at which he is expert. He looked like he needed a cigarette, or a vape, or something else he wasn't allowed to have.

"I'd say it happened last night or evening, 12 to 16 hours ago. Certainly not any more recently."

That was Dr. Arlene Eppensteiner, our hard-working Sussex County coroner, who tries to be at the scene of every unnatural death although Ohio law doesn't require it. She's approximately my age and a foot shorter, with curly dark hair. She was up for re-election, like the county prosecutor, though I was pretty sure even her opponent was voting for her.

"Ms. Quant was struck on her temple by a rock, delivered with great force." Oscar already knew this, but the coroner was telling Mac and me. The EMTs were taking the body to the morgue by the time we arrived. The deceased witch had been found slumped over the table where at times she dealt out tarot cards—including the death card for Mac! A number of said cards were now spread out on the table, some of them splotched with blood. "She was hit as she sat at that table, apparently not able to read her own future in the cards."

"Thanks, Arly," Oscar said.

When she'd departed a few minutes later, the Chief filled us in further: "A woman named Brie Weatherby found the body when she stopped by an hour ago and looked in the window. She said she needed what she called a, quote, 'home healing' from Quant because of, quote 'bad vibes' from a former partner."

Brie Weatherby? Why is that name familiar?

"That is not an unknown phenomenon," Mac informed Oscar. "I have read of individuals who feel 'negative energy' in their domiciles calling in gurus, shamans, or other

energy practitioners to perform a cleansing. Perhaps hellebore is used in the process. The deceased told us it is used in
'purification rituals, warding off negative energies.'"

"Doesn't that sound something like a priest doing a
house blessing?" I asked Mac, trying to be open-minded.

"I suppose," he conceded. "In a broad sense." But he
sounded dubious.

"Anyway," Oscar went on, "Weatherby said she
knew Quant because she'd come to her previously for an af-
ter-hours tarot card reading and was satisfied with the result.
Gibbons is taking her formal statement down at the station
now."

"Wait a minute!" I had it. "Wasn't Brie Weatherby the
woman who got arrested in an environmental protest at the
Shinkle involving the throwing of soup?" Personally, I think
some works of art can only be improved by having food
thrown at them, but it's still illegal and not really likely to save
the ozone layer. And it's safe to say that Adam Mendenhall,
the bowtie-and-suspenders director of the Shinkle Museum
of Art, was not amused.

"She did spend a few hours as a guest in my jail until
her lawyer posted bond," Oscar confirmed. "She got off with
a fine and a warning because the painting was behind glass
and no real harm was done. The museum could never figure
out how she got past the guard with a bag containing cream
of tomato or some such. Clearly, she's got time on her hands
and a few screws loose, but that doesn't mean she's a murderer. Not that we're ruling her out."

"Dr. Eppensteiner called the murder weapon a rock,"
Mac noted. Said weapon had already been bagged and re-

moved by Oscar's officers for forensic review before we arrived. "Was it, in fact, one of those large crystals that Ms. Quant sold for their putative healing properties?"

The Chief shook his head. "No, just a garden variety fossilized sedimentary rock, very common in this part of the country. I'd say the chances of getting fingerprints off it are somewhere south of nil."

"I observed no rocks in the immediate neighborhood or elsewhere in this shop," Mac said. "That means the murderer must have brought it with him or her, which is highly significant."

"How so?" I hated myself for asking.

"Because another word for rock is stone. 'A man or woman who is a medium or a wizard shall be put to death; they shall be stoned with stones, their blood shall be upon them.' That is Holy Writ, the Revised Standard Version's rendering of Leviticus, chapter 20, verse 27. The New American Bible translation renders the passage more directly: 'a medium or fortune-teller shall be put to death by stoning.' And Ms. Quant was, of course, a witch and a fortune teller. The tarot cards on this table, as well as my own experience with her, attest to the latter."

Oscar looked like his head was about to explode. This is not a rarity. He led the way outside, where we stood beneath the **Mistress Quant's Witch's Brew** sign.

"I think you're overthinking this," I told Mac. "It's much more likely that some friend of Braggs made sure that Quant couldn't testify against him. Robin Hauser, for instance. If she lied for Braggs, she could kill for him."

"That's a bit of a stretch on the face of it," Oscar said. "But, yeah, I guess it could be."

"Or perhaps it is just the opposite," Mac offered. "Perhaps someone killed Ms. Quant to give greater credence to her testimony, knowing that the natural assumption would be that she had been killed to silence her."

Oh.

"Either way," I said, "there goes Slade's case for the prosecution. He'll be freaking out so much his comb-over will be askew."

"Of course," Mac rolled on, "this may have nothing to do with the St. Valentine's Day murder at all, and Ms. Quant was killed for an unrelated reason—love, hate, gain, fear. Certainly, she ruffled more than a few feathers with her Instagram channel. Perhaps someone struck her down because of what she did on her channel or fear of what she would do in the future."

"Family members are always good for love, hate, and especially gain, as in money," Oscar pointed out.

"How about professional jealousy?" I offered. "Maybe she was stealing too many of Madam Lena's clients."

I was referring to a local palm reader.

"Didn't Lena close up shop during the COVID shutdown a few years ago?" Oscar asked.

"Well, there you are! Lena's out of business and Quant wasn't. But she is now."

"This speculation is all well and good," Mac said. "However, I persist in thinking that a stone brought in as the murder weapon is a strong indication—"

"Hey, guys!"

That jaunty and familiar greeting came from our favorite working journalist, Johanna Rawls, coming toward us from her silver Prius. Not for nothing do I call her "Tall

Rawls," although not out loud. She stands six feet tall, one inch below me, without her three-inch heels, and she's seldom without them. She's a lovely Nordic type who would not be out of place in a ski resort commercial—slim with long, straight, straw-colored hair, fair skin, and blue eyes. And seeing her reminded me how my plan to talk to Seth, aka The Boyfriend, about the joys of married life had completely gone off-rails because of that stolen e-bike business. I made a mental note to get back to him.

"I heard about the murder on the police scanner," Johanna explained unnecessarily. "Sorry I'm late. Imogene is on her way." That's the staff photographer for the *Observer*, Imogene Casey, with an accent on the "I."

"We'll live," Oscar grunted. But he was just going through the motions. He knows Johanna has a job to do, and she does it well. Accuracy and fairness are never an issue with her, although Oscar might deduct points for aggressiveness.

"So, what's the story?" she asked, old-school reporter's notebook in hand. Sometimes she records interviews, but that spooks Oscar. "Take it from the top, please."

Oscar gave it to her in just-the-facts fashion—when the body was reported, by whom, how Zoraida Quant was killed, the coroner's initial observation that it must have happened last night.

This took a while, and by the time Oscar finished Imogene Casey had arrived. She is short, stocky, and while she doesn't actually smoke, I always think she looks like someone who should be dragging on a cigarette.

We went back into the shop, where Casey took photos of the table with the bloodied tarot cards while Mac thoughtfully rubbed the facial forest that is the McCabe beard. Oscar went on:

"We have, of course, already begun canvassing the area around here, asking if anyone saw anything last night. The trade on this street is not very lively after six o'clock, but a late-working business owner can't be ruled out. And, of course, if any of your readers have any information that might be helpful, we urge them to come forward."

"Do you think it was a robbery gone wrong?" Johanna asked.

"We can't rule that out, but there's no obvious indication of it. The victim had almost a hundred dollars in her purse, and nothing in the shop seems to be disturbed."

Mac hadn't even asked about that. Why would he? If it had been an obvious robbery, Oscar never would have called Mac and I'd be in my office trying to convince Riley St. John that "reached out" is a hackneyed term she should stop using in her social media posts. Along with the overused and unnecessary words "literally" and "definitely." Not to mention "resilient"!

"Also," Oscar continued, "there's no indication of a break-in. Most likely Ms. Quant opened the door for her killer."

"Maybe somebody who didn't want her to testify in the Troy Braggs murder trial?"

Finally, Johanna had put into words what she must have been thinking as soon as she heard the address on the scanner.

"It's too soon to say that," Oscar told her. Although we all knew it wasn't, at least as a strong possibility.

Johanna just looked at him, creating an uncomfortable silence. That's an old journalist trick to get the interviewee to say something to fill the dead air, hoping the "something" will be revealing. But Oscar didn't bite, so Tall Rawls turned to Mac after a half-minute or so. "What are your thoughts?"

"I think Chief Hummel and his men have the situation well in hand."

That's laying it on pretty thick.

"Then why are you here?"

"He knew the victim," Oscar answered for Mac. A classic example of trying to deceive by telling an irrelevant truth! The statement was true but didn't really answer Johanna's question. I was impressed.

"How did that happen?" Johanna asked Mac.

"We had several encounters. Most recently, Ms. Quant performed a tarot reading for me."

Staring, Johanna didn't write that down. "You? You've got to be kidding!"

"It wasn't his idea," I assured her.

With a sigh, my favorite reporter closed her notebook. "Just so you know, gentlemen, I'm not buying that. But I'll be a good girl for now and downplay the 'amateur sleuth on the case' angle in return for you, any of you, calling me day or night when you've got something I can use. Deal?"

"We've got your number," I assured her. She rolled her eyes, which she must have learned from Lynda. In their own charming ways Mac and Oscar signed on to the deal. Johanna departed shortly thereafter, with Casey in tow. As soon as they'd left, Mac said to Oscar:

"When you saw the body, was Ms. Quant's hand reaching toward one of the tarot cards?"

The Chief didn't actually scratch his balding noggin, but if this had been a movie he would have. "I dunno. I didn't exactly focus on that, Mac, what with the bloodied head kind of grabbing my attention."

"Think, man, think!"

"We can look at the crime scene photos. What's pulling your chain?"

"I realized while Ms. Casey was taking photos of the table that the tarot cards are spread out as if Ms. Quant wanted to single out one of them. She may have left us a dying message indicating her killer!"

Chapter Six
The Fool

"THERE WERE FIVE CARDS on the table, all face up," Mac reminded us over sandwiches in Oscar's conference room, which used to be a vault back when the building housed the long-gone Fifth National Bank of Erin. Neither Mac nor Oscar found bloody murder a disincentive for an early lunch.

"And the crime scene photos make it unclear which, if any of them, Quant was pointing to," I said, just to show I was paying attention.

"Which, by the way, there's no reason to think she was," Oscar said around his salami.

Mac nodded. "I do not insist upon it, but it remains a possibility. After all, we have encountered dying clues in previous murders.[6] Drawing her final breaths, after the killer had left and was unable to see what she did with her ebbing strength, Ms. Quant could have attempted to single out a card that would in some way point to her assailant. Therefore, the tarot cards and their meanings are of interest.

"While you two were otherwise occupied"—Oscar with ordering food, me with a few SBU-related calls—"I did some basic research in the tarot, of which I have only minimal knowledge. The cards on the table were all part of what

---

[6] Most recently in the case Jefferson called *The Woman in Red* (MX Publishing, 2023). —*S. McC.*

is called the Major Arcana, which consists of 21 cards out of 78. Every card in the Major Arcana has a number, usually expressed as a Roman numeral. On the table in front of Ms. Quant were The Fool, designated 0; The Magician, I; The Lovers, VI; The Wheel of Fortune, X; and Justice, XX."

"So, you figure that one of those means something in tarot-talk that could point to the killer?" I asked.

"Ah, there's the rub, old boy! Each of these cards is multivalent!"

"Say what?" That was Oscar.

"That's Mac-speak for 'has a lot of different meanings,'" I told him. I know big words; I just don't use them.

"Precisely," Mac agreed. "For example, one source says the Fool indicates folly, mania, extravagance, intoxication, delirium, or frenzy. Those are not all the same. And if the card is reversed, it can mean indecision, hesitation, apathy, or making poor choices."

Oscar wiped his mouth with a paper napkin. "Hell's bells! What you're saying is that it means so much it means nothing at all. That being the case—and given that the crime scene photos don't make it clear that Zoraida Quant was even pointing at one of those tarot things—the only cards I'm interested in right now are the ones being dealt out at my weekly poker game in a few hours."

If Mac heard that, he gave no indication. "There is, however, a simpler possibility," he continued. "Perhaps in her last moments all that caught her attention was the name of the card and its most basic meaning. The Lovers, for example, could refer to the Braggs/Hauser relationship."

"Now you're talking," Oscar enthused. "Ms. Hauser is growing on me as a suspect, given that the most obvious beneficiary of Quant's demise is Hauser's boyfriend."

"Wait a minute!" I interrupted. "When I said if she lied for Braggs, she could kill for him, you called that 'a bit of a stretch.'"

"I've decided there's nothing wrong with stretching—it's good exercise. So, I asked Hauser to pay us a visit this afternoon. She works just a few blocks away from here at Gamble Bank as a teller. Very convenient for her to visit Braggs in jail on her lunch hour, by the way. And I noticed she spent a lot of time talking to Sister Polly, too."

Triple M—aka Sister Polly—is a volunteer chaplain in Oscar's non-volunteer guest house, aka jail, a small facility consisting of a few cells attached to police headquarters.

"Wheel of Fortune could indicate a wealthy person," Mac went on. "Justice might mean a judge; the Fool—well, suffice it to say Jefferson and I heard Ms. Quant use that appellation for certain public servants." *Oscar Hummel and Marvin Slade!*

"The Magician could be you, Mac!" I said, getting into the spirit of it. My brother-in-law still performs what he calls "feats of legerdemain" on an amateur basis, sometimes alone in his office and sometimes before an audience under the uber-hokey moniker of "McCabe the Marvelous, Master of All Mysteries."

"Mac as the killer—I love it!" Oscar enthused.

Mac raised an eyebrow. "The sleuth as murderer has already been done by Agatha Christie."

"But seriously," I said, "this tarot angle is headline stuff. Johanna will be all over it in the *Observer*."

"Only if she finds out about it," Mac said, "and I suggest it would be better that she not. After all, it is only the merest speculation."

"I'm down with that," Oscar said.

ROBIN HAUSER CAME AS a bit of a surprise to me when she showed up a half-hour later in response to Oscar's invitation to "have a little chat." An attractive brunette, about 30, she was well put together in nicely matched office wear, and knew how to not overdo it on the makeup. Her eyes were wide, brown, and didn't seem to miss much. She didn't strike me as a woman who would lie for a loser like Troy Braggs. But, as Lynda has often reminded me, love is irrational.

"What are *they* doing here?" she asked when she entered the conference room with Oscar and saw Mac and me at the table.

"We're the unpaid help," I quipped. No need to add that we were under strict orders to be seen and not heard once Oscar got this party started.

"You're McCabe and Cody," Hauser said.

Well, we couldn't deny that. Mac allowed as how he was pleased to meet her, but she had no time for pleasantries.

"I'm on my lunch hour, so I hope this won't take long," she said. "Anyway, I've already told you everything I know: Troy was with me when that woman says she saw him kill Betty."

"But like I told you on the phone," Oscar said, "there's been a new development in the case. And here it is: Zoraida Quant was found dead this morning. Murdered."

"Murdered!"

If Hauser was acting, she was good at it. But she may have been good at it. The look of surprise on her face certainly seemed like the real thing, quickly followed by the realization of what the news meant.

"Then the only witness against Troy can't testify," Hauser said, almost as if to herself.

"Convenient for your boyfriend, isn't it? Where were you last night?"

"What!"

"It's a simple question." Oscar spread his hands in a gesture meant to be avuncular. It wasn't, but he tried. "And this is just an informal meeting. Of course, you can have a lawyer if you want one, but I was hoping to keep this friendly. With all the time you've spent in my jail visiting Braggs, we aren't exactly strangers."

"Don't play the lawyer card on me," Hauser instructed him. *Another kind of card!* "I have nothing to hide. I was home watching TV, not killing anybody."

She rattled off a list of shows she'd watched on Netflix, Hulu, and Acorn. I'm old enough to remember when that could have been an alibi. Decades ago, there were only four networks, including PBS, and Oscar's counterpart would have asked the suspect to describe the plots of the shows she watched in order to prove that she'd actually been home in front of a 21-inch TV set. But with streaming, she could have watched those programs anytime. (Although the fact that *Fall of the House of Usher* was on her watch list surprised me a little.)

"Were you alone?" Oscar pressed.

"No, Arnold was with me."

Oscar's mug registered surprise and Mac cocked an eyebrow.

"Arnold who?" Oscar pressed.

"Arnold my cat."

We knew a pet psychic who could interview Arnold,[7] but it didn't seem a good idea to bring that up.

I'm pretty sure the Chief counted to 10 silently before he said, "So you can't prove you didn't show up at Quant's shop last evening and smash her head in with a rock?"

You might think Mac would correct that to "stone" to keep it Biblical, but he didn't. Hauser didn't say anything at first either, although she flinched a bit. After a period of Oscar just staring at her—he must have learned that from Johanna—she told him, "I've never been near that place."

"So, the Erin police will not find your fingerprints anywhere in Mistress Quant's Witch's Brew?" Mac clarified, earning a glare from Oscar for speaking.

"No."

That wouldn't necessarily rule out her being there and killing Quant. She could have worn gloves, although that would have looked strange in late summer if anyone had seen her enter the shop that way. On the other hand, if she didn't wear gloves—and maybe the conk on the witch's head was unpremeditated—she would now have trouble claiming that any fingerprints she left behind were from an earlier visit. But wait! Where did the rock/stone come from if the killing wasn't planned in advance? The murder must have been premeditated! (Actually, I'm not sure I thought of that at the time, but I did just now.)

Oscar changed his angle of attack, an old trick to keep the suspect off balance.

"You lied to protect your ex-boyfriend by giving him an alibi for the night he killed your successor in the sack."

---

[7] See *The Magician's Trunk* (MX Publishing, 2024).

This apparently was Oscar's idea of "keeping it friendly." I did like the alliteration, though.

"That's not true." Her eyes shifted, her voice rose, and she was on the edge of losing it. She wasn't a really good liar, in my expert opinion. Good to know.

"If you stick to that fairy tale in court, that's perjury. But bad as that is, murder is far worse. Believe me, you'll feel a lot better if you just admit that you—"

"But I didn't! I didn't, you bastard!"

This last was said in a rising voice that ended in sobs. Oscar had a "let me outta here" expression on his face, but before he could say anything, his executive assistant came into the room. Don't let the pixie-cut copper hair, boyish figure, or penchant for pearl earrings fool you. Holly Burdette has an undergrad degree in business and a master's in criminal justice. Oscar might not be much of an executive, but she's a top-drawer executive assistant.

"Robin!" she said.

"Holly!"

They hugged. This took the "good cop" part of the old "good-cop, bad-cop" routine to a whole new level.

"We're finished here," Oscar said sourly. "For now. Don't leave town, Ms. Hauser."

"WE WERE FRIENDS IN high school, Robin and I," Holly explained later. Their graduation from Malcolm C. Cotton High would have been about a dozen years earlier. "We kind of drifted apart, and one of the reasons is that she always made a fool of herself for the bad boys. Obviously, that hasn't changed. Troy Braggs—yech!"

"A fool!" Mac repeated. But then he shook his massive head. "No, it is simply not credible that the tarot card of that name was meant to indicate her. That is the stuff of fiction." I thought that was a little rich coming from the author of more than 30 mystery novels about a magician named Damon Devlin, many of them involving the "impossible crime" trope.

"Don't ever hug a suspect again," Oscar instructed Holly.

"I'll do my best." Knowing an exit line when she delivered it, she exited.

"You realize that Hauser can't prove she actually streamed those shows that night," I said.

"Sure she can, if she's telling the truth." Oscar said.

"Eh?"

"Her attorney could get a court order for streaming records if she became a serious suspect and felt the need to prove her alibi," Mac said. "The problem with that, of course, is that Netflix or Amazon Prime, for example, could have been streaming into an empty room while Ms. Hauser was at Witch's Brew."

"Then it's a good thing for her that Arnold was there," I said. Exerting myself, I stood up. "I can't sit around here until Zoe Quant shows up." That was the witch's daughter, who had agreed to pay Oscar a visit after identifying her mother's body. "I have work to do back at the office."

I'd touched bases with Popcorn by text, of course, but if I don't show up occasionally the staff forgets what I look like. And I knew from past experience that once Oscar "persuaded" Mac to get involved in a case my absences from the Gamble Building were likely to add up.

With Oscar's skeptical snort in reaction to the word "work" ringing in my ears, I left. Mac followed me out and soon we were climbing into his gas-guzzling 1959 red Chevy convertible. The Macmobile, an ashtray on wheels when Mac is smoking and pondering, has sharklike tail fins and takes up a space-and-a-half compared to a normal car.

"What did you get out of all that, Jefferson?" Mac asked me, once he had piloted us off of Court and onto Main Street.

"A headache. How about you?"

Fortunately, he didn't have to stoke up a cigar to ponder an answer. "Ms. Hauser is so clearly lying when she repeats her alibi for the egregious Mr. Braggs—possibly deluding herself into believing him innocent—that I am almost compelled to believe she is telling the truth about her own activities last night."

"Almost?"

"Well, she does have more at stake when she herself is facing a possible murder charge. That might be an incentive to a better performance than when she is trying to protect her former and possibly future amor."

Soon we were on the SBU campus, but I noticed that we were not heading toward Mac's accustomed parking lot.

"We are making a brief detour to Campus Ministry," he explained when I noted the anomaly. "Oscar mentioned that Ms. Hauser often spoke to Sister Polly while visiting Troy Braggs in jail. I should like to get her perspective."

"ROBIN IS TOTALLY BESOTTED with Troy, of course" was her perspective.

You might think that a religious sister wouldn't know much about besottedness, but you would be wrong. Sister Mary Margaret Malone is a U.S. Army veteran who had at least one serious boyfriend that I know of.[8] She is also in her mid-forties but looks younger, quite cute, with short black hair parted in the middle. (I don't see any gray roots.)

"Do you think she killed Zoraida Quant to keep the witch—no disrespect intended—from testifying against Braggs?" I asked, cutting to the chase.

That warranted a headshake. "I don't sense that Robin is quite that lost yet. And I certainly hope and pray not."

We were sitting in Triple M's cozy campus ministry office, where books on theology mix comfortably on the shelves with horror, science fiction, and fantasy. I thought that a little disorienting until Mac reminded me, in his professorial way, that the fantasy tales of J.R.R. Tolkien and his pal C.S. Lewis are thoroughly rooted in theology. And don't even get Triple M started on that whole Superman-as-Moses thing!

"I presume you suggested to her she should tell the truth about the night Betty Erlanger died, both in the name of justice and to clear her own conscience," Mac told her.

Before I had a chance to tell the big guy that Sherlock Holmes or Nero Wolfe never presume anything, Triple M said:

"It wouldn't be ethical for me to comment on that, even though Robin and I aren't technically in a counseling relationship." She managed to make that not sound like a rebuke. "But I think I can say this much because it's obvious: Robin Hauser is under Troy Braggs's spell." *Witchcraft!* "And unless that spell gets broken, he's going to ruin her life. If he hasn't already."

---

[8] See *The* 1895 *Murder* (MX Publishing, 2012).

Chapter Seven

Round Up the Unusual Suspects

BACK AT THE OFFICE, Popcorn was her usual restrained self.
"What happened, Boss? Dish!"

"I was with Oscar the whole time," I told her.
"Ask him!"

She pretended to pout. "He never tells me anything."

"Lips too busy?"

Apparently, that wasn't even worth a dirty look.

"All I know is what you said when you ran out of here
this morning—'Ding Dong! The witch is dead.' Which was
kind of cold, by the way."

That wasn't strictly true, the part about it being all she
knew. I'd sent a quick text clarifying that Zoraida Quant had
been stoned to death and that I likely would be playing
hookey for a while. Now that I was back, I filled her in. Then
she filled me in on what our two staff members were up to.
Having nothing more urgent on my afternoon plate, I visited
each of them for a little face time, just enough to remind them
I was in theoretical charge without getting in their way.

"Our followers on X are up by 3,000 over a year ago,"
magenta-hair-and-pigtailed Riley St. James reported. "You
saw my tweets"—the term endures even though the platform
is no longer called Twitter—"on GK's NPR appearance.
Lots of feedback, mostly positive."

Sylvester Link was working on the next issue of *Ben*, our alumni mag, and struggling a bit in his role as advisor to our student newspaper, *The Spectator*, where he was a reporter in his student years. In those days, I tagged him as "Serious Sylvester," although not out loud.

"I just don't feel like I relate to today's students," he complained. Link no longer wears a suit every day, but somehow always looks like he's wearing one anyway.

"Don't worry about it," I said. "You didn't relate to yesterday's students either. Just kidding." *Not really.* "Seriously, it's a different world. Just try to understand those budding journalists before you try to make them understand you." Good line! I made a mental note to use it again.

To round out the fun, late afternoon brought a budget meeting with Lesley Saylor-Mackie, my immediate boss in her dual role of executive vice president and provost of SBU. An eminent historian and expert on Ohio native William Howard Taft, she also displays an admirable ability to squeeze pennies until Abe cries. Not that you would know it from her Gamble Building office, which is almost as elegant as she is. But she inherited that from her predecessor, Ralph Pendergast, about whom more later.

We went over the numbers, at one point going down a side alley in which we marveled at how things had changed since we'd each come to work here so many years earlier. In those days, it had been much smaller, known as St. Benignus College, and presided over by the late, truly great Fr. Joseph Pirelli, of blessed memory.

"So," she said. She sat back and assumed a casual posture, which put me on alert. Saylor-Mackie is in her late 60s, with dignified gray hair, hazel eyes, and a full wardrobe of business suits. Casual is not her main vibe. She was a highly successful mayor of Erin before reaching her current SBU position. Now she's studiously uninvolved in partisan politics, but that doesn't mean she isn't political. In the best possible sense, of course. "How's Mac?"

"Mac is . . . Mac. Why do you ask?" My brother-in-law is already a tenured full professor, which means that Saylor-Mackie could neither help nor hurt him except in the most extraordinary of circumstances. But then, nothing is ordinary about Sebastian McCabe.

"Because GK asked me. You know what a childish delight he takes in Mac's adventures."

"Nobody's perfect."

She almost smiled.

"But as for adventures, he's in the thick of a new one. I'm sure you remember that eccentric city council candidate last year named Zoraida Quant."

"The witch?"

"Got it in one! Well, she's now a late witch. Mac called me this morning . . ."

LATE THAT AFTERNOON, MAC and I were back in Oscar's office, waiting for Quant's daughter to drop by.

"Let us not hesitate to be creative in our speculations as to the identity of the killer," Mac said. "We have had more than our share of outside-the-box solutions in previous cases."

"What's wrong with Hauser as the killer?" Oscar demanded from behind his curved wooden desk. "Too obvious for you?"

"I do not believe that Ms. Hauser is lying when she denies killing Zoraida Quant any more than I believe she is telling the truth with her alibi for Troy Braggs."

"And what makes you a human lie detector?"

"More than thirty years in academia," I suggested.

"I could be wrong," Mac conceded, not really believing it. "However, there are many other suspects that should be explored, plausible or otherwise. The woman who found the body, for example—Brie Weatherby."

"Hardly a model citizen," I reminded Oscar. "As you well know from hosting her in your jail after that soup-throwing protest at the Shinkle."

"Some of the fingerprints we found in Quant's wacky shop were hers," Oscar conceded, "but you would expect that of a client, customer, whatever." He chugged coffee.

"Which brings to mind the possibility of other clients the victim may have had after hours," Mac riposted. "Do we know of any?"

"Funny you should ask. My crack team"—probably Gibbons—"overlooking nothing, found a print calendar hanging on the wall. Lots of cute photos of cats each month, by the way. Weatherby's name and two others show up on various dates over the past few months, always in the evening, with the word 'tarot' and a time next to them. It didn't take a Sherlock Holmes"—*oh, come on!*—"to figure out that they were all appointments for Quant to do her tarot card reading thing."

"The other names?"

"Jade Lazelle and Dixie Parks."

"There's a server at Bobbie McGee's named Jade," I recalled. "That's an unusual name, so it could be her." The name Parks also rang a faint bell with me, but not paired with the less-than-common first name of Dixie.

"You figure one of those women didn't like the looks of the future Quant was serving up, and so she brained the bearer of bad news?" Oscar asked Mac. His voice dripped with so much sarcasm that I thought his shirt would get wet.

"I figure nothing, Oscar; I am merely collecting data. In fact, it strikes me that the targets of Ms. Quant's Instagram channel would be far more likely to be so offended as to take extreme action."

Oscar got an *"even Gibbons didn't think of going down that alley"* look on his face.

"And who would that be, these targets?"

"I created an Instagram account this afternoon so that I could find out. Ms. Quant's channel, by the way, is called 'WitchCrafty.' Her approach was entirely negative, and her victims were all public persons of some stature in the community. The mayor, for example."

"Whatever for?" came out of my mouth without permission from my brain. Reverend Fred Sutterlee, mayor of Erin and senior pastor of the Apostolic Holiness Church of the Holy Spirit, is the most inoffensive of men. I mean that in a good way, not in the sense of inoffensive because he never did anything.

"She reviled the good Reverend for being, simultaneously, a man of the cloth and an elected official. She contended—inaccurately, in my view—that his dual roles violate the hallowed principle of church and state separation. Her other video targets included Ralph Pendergast and Carson Kincade for their involvement in the highly contentious Underground Railroad Festival . . ."

Erin's history as a major stop on the Underground Railroad, being right across the river from Kentucky, is a point of local pride. Mac's house at 23 Half Moon Street is one of dozens that were stations on the railroad. Count me among those surprised when the festival dreamed up by the local Convention & Visitors Bureau was condemned by a small but vocal group of non-residents who condemned it for demonstrating a "white savior mentality." People stayed away in droves, which I thought was due not so much to the negative publicity as to under-marketing and the fact that many of the Ohio and Kentucky history buffs likely to be interested had already been to Erin to see the historic homes involved.

". . . the county auditor, Mallory Ziv, for the increase in property taxes . . ." Mac continued.

"I'd join that protest," Oscar said.

"You wouldn't protest at the price you could get for your house today, given the way values have shot up because of the inventory shortage," I countered.

Wait a minute! I'm defending a tax increase!

". . . Marvin Slade, apparently just on general principles, given that his record of successful prosecutions is an excellent one . . ."

Oscar chortled. Yes, I know people don't really chortle, but Oscar did. "Erica must have loved that—and reposted it everywhere she could."

"Don't be so sure about that," I said. "Remember, that pair have occasionally been seen together outside the courtroom in recent months. I think they're having a truce or something." The "or something" was the interesting part, but who am I to speculate?

Erica Slade, a former Cincinnati Bengals cheerleader, became a defense lawyer explicitly to battle her ex in court. Now she's the premier such attorney in town—"hell on high heels," I like to say—although she often has to settle for a plea deal because, you know, the client is guilty. As to whether she was glad or sad not to be Troy Braggs's barrister, the jury was still out in my mind. It was a high-profile case well beyond Erin, which she would love, but it had been looking like a slam dunk for the prosecution—until this morning.

". . . and Madam Lena, whom she accused of being, quote, 'a fake, a phony, and a fraud'—which is a double redundancy," Mac finished.

Madam Lena! I knew it!

"I don't see how any of those highly respectable citizens fit into your fantasy about those tarot cards being a clue to the killer," Oscar said.

"The Fool, the Magician, the Lovers, the Wheel of Fortune, and Justice," Mac mused. "By thunder, I must admit that no unique link suggests itself, but that may be because we do not know enough about her relationships with the targets of her video ire. Presumably she would regard almost any of them as fools, but that would be unhelpful."

"On the other hand," I said, "maybe if there is a clue in the tarot cards it's not in any one card but in all of them."

Mac saw it right away. "Indeed, Jefferson! If one takes tarot cards as a general symbol for telling the future, they could point to Ms. Quant's competitor—or, rather, former competitor—Madam Lena, the palm reader."

Chapter Eight
The Death Doula

HOLLY BURDETTE POPPED IN with some welcome news:

"Zoe Quant is here, Chief. I put her in the conference room. But I didn't hug her."

Mac raised an eyebrow at Oscar. "Your executive assistant implies that she considers the younger Ms. Quant a suspect."

"She's just playing with my head," was Oscar's take.

"But she could have something there," I said. "Zoe probably inherits."

"And matricide is not unknown," Mac added.

Maybe we were just playing with Oscar's head. I wasn't sure.

I DON'T KNOW WHAT I expected from Zoe Quant, but I didn't get it.

She was in her mid-to-late thirties, with hair about the same shade of red as mine, courtesy of Clairol or some such, and done up in a Mohawk style. Her lips, earrings, the frames of her glasses, and her low-heeled shoes were all equally scarlet, but her dress—a body-hugging number made of some soft material—was cream colored.

Oscar began by thanking her for coming in and then expressing his sympathy, adding: "I'm sorry I had to ask you to come here right after identifying your mother. Death of a loved one is never easy, and unnatural death—murder most of all—is especially difficult." This was a kinder, gentler Oscar Hummel than I was used to. Maybe he was mellowing. But probably not.

"Thank you, Chief," the bereaved said, "but death is my business. I'm a certified thanatologist and death doula."

"Come again?"

"Thanatology is the scientific practice of studying death and the various attitudes towards death, including the bereavement process," she said.

"Of course," Mac said. "I confess, however, that I am unfamiliar with the adjective 'death' preceding the noun 'doula,' which is usually an individual supporting a pregnant woman through labor."

Zoe Quant nodded her Mohawked head. "The principle is the same. I am there to help the transitioning person and family find light at what can be a very dark time. I help them deal with death." The word "dealing" made me think of tarot cards, but not for long. "I usually enter the picture when death is clearly on the horizon—not unexpected, as it was with Zoraida. I am not always there at the end, but I was with my client Melina Crawford when Zoraida transitioned." *Alibi noted!* "I also blog, teach online, and lecture throughout the country on how to handle death and loss."

While Mac raised an eyebrow, Oscar cleared his throat to signal the pleasantries were over. "Obvious question: Who might want your mother dead?"

"Who knows? The world is full of looney-tunes."

"I just thought you might have some insight, since your name was in her wallet as an emergency contact." That was surprisingly practical of the elder Quant, I thought.

"That's why we asked you to identify the body. Who benefits under your mother's will?"

"Are you asking me as Zoraida's daughter or as her executrix?"

Referring to her mother by first name was something I was getting used to, but with difficulty. Plus, I was surprised she used the feminine "executrix."

The Chief shrugged. "Whichever one can answer the question without asking any more questions." *A comeback worthy of Sebastian McCabe!*

Zoe crossed her legs with strategic precision. "Actually, I didn't know the answer in either capacity until I looked at the will a few hours ago. My brother and I inherit equally, and there is a lot to inherit. Zoraida was an Applewhite, not rich like the Gambles and the Harridans, but rich enough. And she wasn't a big spender."

"Did I detect a note of, perhaps, disdain when you mentioned your brother?" Mac asked.

She gave that a think. "That's fair, I suppose. Zane and I live on different philosophical planets, you might say. He thinks he's a rationalist; I think he's rationalizer."

Mac must be loving all this wordplay.

"You didn't mention your father in regard to the will," Oscar pointed out. "Is he deceased?"

"Honestly, I don't know for sure. He may be by now. Russell Quant walked out on us about fifteen years ago, when I was in my late teens. Zoraida told us that he was dead, and I guess he was to her. That's when I became interested in thanatology and Zoraida started dabbling in Wicca. She was a true believer, you know; the witch identity wasn't just part of a business plan. I myself embrace no particular belief system and dismiss none. Whatever works for you. Zane, on the other hand, dismisses them all, or thinks he does. He is under the illusion that his beliefs aren't beliefs; they're facts.

"Anyway, I was well into my twenties before Zoraida let it slip that as far as she knew our father was still alive. Her excuse for lying all those years was that if he didn't care enough about his children to reach out to them, she thought it would be less painful for us to think he was dead. She had a point, I suppose."

The bearded McCabe phiz gave no clue as to what, if anything, he made of all that. I set it down as an interesting rabbit hole, but nothing more.

"We are aware that your late mother was a bit of a prickly personality," Mac told Zoe Quant. A finer example of understatement I had never heard. "Other than the targets of her Instagram channel, can you think of anyone else who had a serious animosity toward her?"

This was "Who might want your mother dead?" repackaged.

Zoe crossed her legs in the other direction, giving her time to decide whether to say it. Then she said it:

"This may take you down a blind alley"—*been there, done that, already have enough T-shirts!*—"but there's a local reverend named Adam Sapp who has his own Instagram channel where he said that witches should be stoned. Zoraida told me about it. She said he didn't mention her by name, but that she was clearly who he had in mind."

Chapter Nine
Bewitching News

THAT EVENING, VIEWERS OF Prime News Network's long-running *American Scene* program were treated to veteran reporter Bennington Lee—you know him: a tall black man with shaved head, goatee, and tailored suit—walking the streets of Erin. PNN has changed a lot over the years, but both Lee and *American Scene* are much the same as they were when they first visited Erin almost a decade earlier.[9]

As usual, the segment was a combination of live reporting and material taped earlier. It began with Lee standing outside Witch's Brew, which looked suitably eerie in the late summer twilight.

"Once again, the small community of Erin in southwest Ohio has been rocked by a murder. And this time"—dramatic pause—"the victim is a self-proclaimed witch."

Lee brought viewers around America up to speed on the basic facts of who Quant was, in case they hadn't seen the Associated Press story by AP veteran Morrie Kindle or the 90 seconds on the evening news. This part of the report was illustrated by still photos of the dead woman, along with

---

[9] See *Erin Go Bloody* (MX Publishing, 2016).

what's called "B-roll"—video without sounds—of the murder scene by daylight. Then came an interview with the woman who found the body.

"I needed a home healing from Mistress Quant—that's what she called herself—to deal with some negative energy there," she explained. "Now her own shop is going to need a healing big time!"

The *American Scene* producers must live for quotes like that.

Brie Weatherby appeared to be in her seventies, with long gray hair. Wearing a plaid shirt and jeans, she didn't look like somebody who patronized a witch at a metaphysical supply shop. Or like somebody who threw soup at paintings in a gallery, for that matter. She appeared to be comfortably ensconced in her home as she spoke to Bennington Lee.

"What were your emotions upon finding the body?" he wondered.

"Shock, most of all."

The video switched back to Lee, looking sympathetic, or concerned, or something. Then to Weatherby again.

"The head was a bloody mess," she went on, apparently untraumatized enough to talk about it.

Lee informed the viewers, via voice over B-roll, that Quant had been struck by a rock—not mentioning the Biblical injunction to stone witches, which surely meant he didn't know about it.

Only then did he note that the deceased had been scheduled to be a key witness in a murder trial.

"That should have come in the first ten seconds—it's the most important thing!" Lynda instructed me. "Newspaper old-timers call that 'burying the lede,' when the reporter puts a vital fact way down in the story." This I knew. "Have I ranted about how often that happens these days?"

"Many times. I think it's very cute of you."

Then came video segments of the dueling lawyers.

Marvin Slade, county prosecutor: "This brutal crime will not prevent us from convicting Troy Braggs of the murder of an innocent woman who loved him. We have Ms. Quant's sworn statement, and it will be presented to the jurors in the Braggs trial."

"Note how he subtly suggested that Quant was killed to keep her from talking," I told Lynda.

"That wasn't so subtle."

Phoebe Farleigh, defense counsel: "Ms. Quant's murder was horrific, but neither my client nor anyone associated with him had anything to do with it."

"How could she know that?" Lynda objected. "It's not like some pal of Braggs who decided to do in the eyewitness would tell the lawyer first."

"She's on autopilot, doing what a defense lawyer does. It would seem strange if she didn't."

At this point, Bennington Lee pivoted back to the Brie Weatherby interview.

"What was Mistress Quant like?"

"She was a wonderful tarot reader. I didn't really know her that well on a personal level."

Lee attempted to give a sense of the victim by showing a few excerpts from her social media account on X, and a quick hit from an Instagram video in which she called Madam Lena "a fake, a phony, and a fraud who wouldn't know the Major Arcana from the Minor Arcana."

Then followed some B-roll of the Mulberry Street neighborhood by day, with Lee's voice telling us it was near the public library and populated by small shops. Bruce Gordon, long-time city councilman and operator of a flower shop near Witch's Brew, allowed as how the murder was "disturbing" but (cliché alert) "not who we are."

The report ended, as it began, with Lee live on camera. "We reached out to Erin Police Chief Oscar Hummel, but he declined to go on camera. He did say, quote, 'The murder of Zoraida Quant is our highest priority, and will continue to be until the killer is identified, arrested, convicted, and sentenced.' This is Bennington Lee, on the American scene tonight in Erin, Ohio."

Lynda and I aren't regular viewers of that program, but Oscar had alerted me that this was coming. In fact, if you were to speculate that he asked my advice on how to respond to a PNN request for an interview, you would not be wrong.

About an hour later, we were watching Cincinnati's TV4 Action News on our bedroom TV. Rumor has it that co-anchors Brian Rose and Tammie Tucker have become more than friendly out of office hours, so Lynda likes to look for signs of that. Rose, whose horn-rim glasses are something of a trademark, led the way with:

"Good evening. The Ohio River town of Erin has been rocked"—*bad choice of words, Brian!*—"by the slaying of a woman expected to be the key prosecution witness in the trial of Troy Braggs, accused of a dramatic murder by arrow last Valentine's Day."

"He didn't bury the lead," I commented.

From there Rose turned the report over to reporter Mandy Peters who, like Bennington Lee before her, was hanging around outside Witch's Brew for the live part of her report. "Yes, Brian," she began, "self-proclaimed witch and tarot card reader Zoraida Quant was found dead this morning . . ." She gave a good summary of the facts as known.

The energetic Ms. Peters—whom I've known since she was an intern reporter with roots the same color as her hair—managed to catch Oscar on the way out the door to his Wednesday night card game. Except for the deer-caught-in-the-headlights look at the beginning, which Peters could have left on the proverbial cutting room floor, the Chief did okay. He noted that the investigation was just beginning and managed to stop himself from saying "we'll catch the bastard," while making it clear that's what he meant.

After Oscar's 20 seconds of fame, Peters came back to remind viewers that the murder trial had put a new focus on Marvin Slade's profile as a "tough-on-crime" prosecutor. He and Braggs's counsel for the defense were both only too happy to talk to her as they had to Lee, saying much the same in less time because this was a report of under three minutes total. That opened the door for the part where the co-anchor asks a question that the reporter pretends is spontaneous.

"And that trial will continue?" Rose asked.

"Yes, but we don't know when," Peters informed us. "The prosecutor has asked the judge for a continuance because of the evolving situation."

This hadn't been covered in Slade's taped comments.

"We'll be following developments closely," Rose assured us.

The camera switched to the other side of the anchor desk and the always-perky Tammie Tucker, Rose's presumed off-camera squeeze.

"The Altiora Corp., with far-flung operations in a host of different cities, announced today that it is expanding in southwest Ohio with . . ."

This I knew from former Altiora exec Grant Kingsley. Our SBU president still has connections at the Hartford, Connecticut company, which is one of the last of the great conglomerates since the old General Electric broke up.

". . . several hundred white collar jobs over the next eighteen months."

At this point Lynda snuggled closer to me, and I sort of lost track of whoever was saying whatever on the TV. *Oh, those chocolate brown eyes with flakes of gold! That cutely crooked nose and beautiful oval face! The generous curves of her . . .*

"Are you, um, sleepy?" she asked after a little while.

"Not anymore."

"Neither am I, *tesoro mio.* Neither am I."

I turned off the TV.

SOMETIME LATER, LYNDA sat up in bed.

"Zoe Quant's father, what's-his-name!" she exclaimed.

"Russell Quant. What about him?"

"I bet he really is dead, and Zoraida Quant killed him. He's probably buried in her basement. That's what would happen in one of Mac's books. And it would be great for the podcast I'm going to make out of this. Maybe I can call it 'The Witch Is Dead.'"

"But who killed her, Lyn?"

"Her son or daughter, or both, realizing that they'd been deprived of father-love all those years."

"That's very creative," I praised, "but it doesn't expand the suspect list any. Those two are already under the magnifying glass as heirs to Zoraida."

"Oh. Well, even better, then—Russell Quant is actually alive, and *he* killed her!"

"That sounds even more like one of Mac's fairy tales. You should be a mystery writer."

And yet, it wasn't a bad idea.

Chapter Ten
"Shall Be Stoned"

KEY WITNESS MURDERED! screamed the obvious headline
in Thursday's *Observer* above the story and a four-column
crime scene photo courtesy of Imogene Casey. Looking at
our three adorable (when not frustrating) offspring dawdling
over their Cheerios, I was glad they couldn't read those words
or what followed in Johanna's story:

> Zoraida Quant, 68, who was scheduled to be
> the major prosecution witness in the just-begun
> trial of Troy Braggs for the murder of former
> girlfriend Betty Erlanger, was found bludgeoned
> to death on Wednesday morning in her Mistress
> Quant's Witch's Brew shop on Mulberry Street.
>
> Erin Police Chief Oscar Hummel said
> Quant, a self-proclaimed witch and former city
> council candidate, was apparently struck repeat-
> edly by a rock found at the scene, although offi-
> cial postmortem results have not been released
> by the coroner's office.
>
> Brie Weatherby, 76, a patron of the store,
> discovered the body and called 911.
>
> Hummel said there were no signs of a rob-
> bery.

"We have, of course, already begun canvassing the area . . ."

"I'm glad Oscar talked to Johanna," Lynda said.

"That's called cultivating the local press."

"Is that what you were doing with me when we first
met, darling?"

"No comment."

At the bottom of the story, where it jumped from
page one, there was what is known in the trade as a "refer
line"—a few words referring the reader to Ben Silverstein's
story about the second day of the Troy Braggs trial ("Jurors
Hear Coroner Testimony, p. 3A").

THE NEWSPAPER WAS ON Popcorn's desk when I arrived at
the office, showing signs of wear even though she'd already
had all the gory details from me and, presumably, her beloved
Oscar. After giving me five minutes to get oriented, she
brought me my cup of decaf and settled in her familiar chair.

"So, what's on your 'to do' list today that I'm going
to wind up doing?" she asked.

"What do you mean?"

"I mean that in a few minutes Mac's going to call, and
then you're going to run out of here on some murder-related
business, checking in with me occasionally, completely confident that your assistant director will manage both your staff
and your bosses while you're gone."

"Oh." I couldn't argue with that; after all, it was true.
"Well, it should be a quiet day in the office until the first crisis. Riley—"

My cell rang. Popcorn waved goodbye on her way out.

"Lynda has a theory," I told Mac by way of greeting. "Russell Quant killed his ex-wife!"

"Good morning, Jefferson! Does the good Lynda posit why he emerged to do so at this particular time? Or at all?"

I didn't think of that.

"You can work out the fine points," I told him.

"Well, that is a thought. Meanwhile, I have prevailed upon Colonel Gibbons to let us sit in on his interview with Reverend Sapp, the pastor who referred to stoning witches on his Instagram channel. Please meet me in the parking lot in ten minutes."

"I'll see you in fifteen."

Sometimes I have to assert myself.

REVEREND ADAM SAPP lived in a 1950s-era brick ranch home in a middle-income neighborhood. The bushes were neatly trimmed, and the grass was cut.

We met Gibbons outside.

"Thank you for tolerating our presence," Mac told him, and I thought the verb was a good one.

"None of the fingerprints found inside Witch's Brew are Robin Hauser's," Gibbons said by way of catching us up.

"Which still doesn't exclude her because she could have worn gloves," I said, just to be helpful.

"Noted."

Sapp was blond-haired, baby-faced, probably under the age of 30, wearing jeans and a white polo shirt. And he looked familiar. Just as Gibbons finished introducing us and explaining why we were there ("unofficial consultants"), I figured out where I'd seen him before.

"You're an EMT," I blurted out, although he knew that. He'd been on the scene of a previous murder to which we had been called, although I couldn't remember which one.

"Yeah, I'm on night shift now," he said. "I thank the Lord I wasn't on duty when Ms. Quant's body was discovered. What a horrible thing! You said you wanted to talk to me about her, but you didn't make it clear why. Come on into my study."

The study wasn't quite what I expected from his kind of clergyman, being dominated by a large poster of a garage band called Easy Times. On closer look, I saw that the drummer was Reverend Adam Sapp. It struck me that a garage band was a far cry, musically speaking, from A Joyful Noise, the trio of tenors made up of Reverend Mayor Fred Sutterlee, a Protestant pastor; Father Francis Xavier O'Boyle, a Catholic priest; and Rabbi David Goldman.

"I understand that you're the pastor of a small non-denominational church," Gibbons began. Oscar's right-hand man is average in everything but ability and has a poker face even when he's not playing poker. So, I knew this was going somewhere.

"That's right," Sapp acknowledged. *EMT? Check. Garage band drummer? Check. Pastor? Check.* "It's called The Journey. We meet in that closed Dollar Tree on Cherry Street." This was quite a different kettle of fish (as my dad would say) from Glad Tidings, the local megachurch with a contemporary vibe and its name on the stadium where the minor league Erin Eagles baseball team plays. "What's that got to do with Ms. Quant?"

"Your church has an Instagram channel. On that channel are several videos in which you call for witches to be stoned. Zoraida Quant was a witch, and she was stoned. So maybe you can see why we'd be interested in talking to you." This was a long speech by Gibbons's standards.

Sapp did a pretty good imitation of that Edvard Munch painting, *The Scream*, without actually screaming or putting his hands to his head.

"I didn't call for stoning anybody!" He didn't quite shout. "I was just citing Holy Scripture to make the point that the occult is not to be trifled with. Heck, Father Juan agrees with me!"

"Of that I have no doubt!" Mac affirmed.

Father Juan Diego Ortega, Triple M's boss in his capacity as director of campus ministries, is an exorcist who has stories of strange happenings from his own experience that would make Oscar's hair stand on end if he had any.[10]

"Witchcraft and divination are condemned throughout the Bible," Sapp continued. "Look what happened to Saul when he visited the Witch of Endor."[11]

"And what about stoning?" Gibbons pressed, ignoring King Saul's fate. "Did some of those passages you quoted from the Bible involve stoning?" Gibbons was asking a question to which he had the answer. And I knew from the briefing before this little confab that Sapp on Instagram had rolled out some of the same passages to which Mac treated us at Quant's shop the morning before.

---

[10] See *No Ghosts Need Apply* (MX Publishing, 2021).

[11] The story is told in 1 Samuel 28:3–25. —*S. McC.*

"Well, yes." Sapp looked miserable. "But only to make the point that God takes this stuff seriously and so should we."

"And then there was Exodus 22:18," Gibbons added. "You quoted that: 'You shall not let a sorceress live.'"

Sapp had no response. Privately, I was thinking that "sorceress" sounds a lot cooler than "witch."

"I noted that your Instagram posts have received a substantial number of views for a small church in a small town," Mac said.

"I feel like it's my mission to engage the culture, so I do lots of social media." Then the implication of Mac's comments hit him. "You don't think somebody killed her because of one of my videos, do you? Lord have mercy, I sure hope not!"

"Social media inspire people to do a lot of things they shouldn't," I offered. That didn't seem to help.

"I didn't mention Ms. Quant by name, but the name Witch's Brew might have come up." *That would be a clue, all right.*

"Actually, it didn't," Gibbons said. The man has an incurable fetish for accuracy.

Mac pivoted: "How did you come to know about Zoraida Quant, Reverend?"

"Call me Adam. She made a big splash in the city council race last year. Remember her slogan, 'Put some charm into city council'? As in occult charms? I was *praying* for Ms. Quant, not wishing her any evil. I wanted her to change her ways, not die. She was as far from God as her son is, just in a different way."

Mac raised an eyebrow.

"You know Zane Quant?"

"Years ago, I did. He taught me science in middle school, and it was pretty clear that science was his only god—he liked to think of himself as a rationalist. I can't believe that he got along with his mother very well."

"Where were you on Tuesday evening?" That was Gibbons asking, but I was pretty sure he was just dotting an "i" or crossing a "t" in his usual thorough manner.

"Practicing with my fellow band members, from late afternoon through evening. We have a gig this weekend. I'll give you their names."

WE MET ZANE QUANT at the Erin Historical Society, during his early lunch hour, because he didn't want us to show up at Hope Farmer Middle School. The society is housed in an old train station next door to the school, and I got the impression that Quant sometimes hung out there to listen to the quiet.

"I've had very little contact with my mother for several years," the male Quant wanted us to know as soon as we'd all seated ourselves at a big round table for visitors. "So, I don't see how I can be of any help." He was thin and mostly bald—like a young Professor Moriarty without the charm, Mac said later.

"Just routine," Gibbons assured him. "Do you have any idea who might want to kill your mother?"

He shook his head. "If you mean a name, no. She was a harmless nutball. I assume she was killed by a nutball who wasn't harmless. I know she posted a lot of wacky stuff on social media. My friends were more than happy to keep me informed about that." I could almost hear the quote marks around "friends" through the irony in his voice.

"Why had you been out of contact with your mother?" Mac pressed.

Quant sighed. "Let's just say that I am a very different person from my mother and my sister in that I am a rational human being. I believe in what can be seen, touched, and measured by science. I do not believe in spirits, heaven and hell, predicting the future, or any of that rot."

It's not everybody who can use the word "rot" in a conversation without sounding like a BBC show, so I gave Quant points for that. But I had to ask:

"If you two were so detached, how come you were in your mother's will?"

He did a good job of looking surprised. Either that, or he was surprised. "I am?"

"Your sister didn't tell you?" Gibbons asked.

"I haven't talked to her in years. She left a message on my phone about our mother's death, but I didn't get around to calling her back."

Waiting for hell to freeze over? Oh, I forgot! You don't believe in hell.

"Just for the record, where were you the night your mother was killed?" Gibbons asked.

"I was at a school open house most of the evening, then had a few drinks with some fellow teachers. After dealing with parents for two hours, we needed it!"

"Their names?"

Quant rattled them off, almost as if he'd been ready.

Chapter Eleven
The Three Clients

GIBBONS WENT BACK TO the police station after that pair of interviews, but Mac had other ideas for us. He wanted to talk to the three women who appeared on Zoraida Quant's calendar as scheduled for tarot card readings in recent weeks. Oscar and Gibbons didn't think them worthy of city employees' time, and Mac was fine with us going duo.

"The Three Clients," he mused as we settled into his land yacht.

"I'd call them customers."

"I feel sure that Ms. Quant called them clients. *The Three Clients* could have been the title of a Nero Wolfe book." Since I'm a Wolfean, Mac didn't have to spell out what he meant: Many of the Wolfe books have "three" in the title because they're collections of three novellas each: *Three Witnesses*, *Three Men Out*, *Three Doors to Death*, etc. "Of course, there was already the Wolfe novel *Too Many Clients.*"

"Of course."

JADE LAZELLE, AS I'D SUSPECTED, was the server at Bobbie McGee's Sport Bar named Jade. We confirmed that when we dropped in there for lunch and strategically arranged to be sitting in her area of service.

"Are we expecting anyone else today?" she asked in a chipper server-voice as she handed us menus.

"Not unless our many fans find out we're here," I quipped.

"Perfect."

I'm not sure why servers say "we"—it's not like they're eating with us—but that seems to be universal these days. As is the word "perfect."

Lazelle was a stout woman of medium height, probably in her early fifties, who didn't dye her graying blonde hair, which I respected.

It would be tedious for you, dear reader, if I were to describe the process of ordering drinks (Caffeine-Free Diet Coke for me vs. caffeinated coffee for Mac) and food (tuna salad vs. triple cheeseburger with heart-attack fries), and then consuming same, so I will present in one continuous narrative a dialogue that was in fact stretched out during the ordering, serving, and eating process.

When she came back to deliver the drinks and take our orders, Lazelle opened a door that Mac dove right through.

"Aren't you that Sebastian Whozits who's always getting mixed up in murders and such?"

"McCabe," he informed her, "and I have indeed had the honor to be of some assistance to the Erin police. In fact, currently—"

Lazelle's face darkened and she interrupted. "Well, I hope you help them catch the bastard who whacked Zoraida Quant. That woman saved me."

"How so?"

I don't know why Mac asked. There was no way she was *not* going to tell us.

"I was in a bad place after I lost my husband a few months back," Lazelle said. "It was always just the two of us. I don't have many other friends and relatives, no kids. But Mistress Quant read the cards and opened up all kinds of possibilities for me even though we only had that one session, a couple of weeks ago."

"What happened?" I asked.

"She turned over the Wheel of Fortune card and told me that could mean a change. And for me, a change could only mean improvement. But she also told me that I could make my future, not be a victim of it. That I had that power if only I would tap into it."

Mac arched an eyebrow, and I could guess why. The Wheel of Fortune! That was one of the cards on the table in front of Quant when she died, a possible dying message. Or maybe Mac was just reacting to the banality of the witch's statement.

"And how, may I ask, has your life improved?" Mac asked.

"For one thing, I applied for a job at Ricoletti's Ristorante, where the tips are better, and I got it. This is my last week here." She smiled. Then she frowned. "I hated to tell Ms. McGee, though. She's so nice. But she congratulated me." Lazelle smiled again. "And another thing that happened, Serena Mason gave me a fifty-dollar tip. I was going to use the money to buy sessions with Mistress Quant soon. Instead, I'm saving up to buy a dog."

Serena Mason is herself a wheel of fortune. Not only the richest but also one of the nicest citizens of Erin, she bought the *Erin Observer & News-Ledger* from Grier Newspaper Group a few years back just to preserve local ownership. Then she set up a trust that will inherit the paper and keep it going after she's gone. In other words, Serena spreading her wealth around was no rare event. Even I could have predicted that! But, of course, the Wheel of Fortune card didn't predict anything, except to a believer who read it retroactively.

Mac got down to the business that brought us there. "Did you see or hear anything during your session with Mistress Quant that now strikes you as significant in view of her murder?"

"Like what?" Lazelle wondered.

"Anything out of the ordinary"—*for a witch*—"that might explain why someone wanted to kill her."

"Oh, gosh, no."

"Do you know any of Mistress Quant's other customers—or clients, if you prefer?"

"Maybe. I'm sure that people go in and out of that store all the time. I think I saw Phil Oakland, the locksmith, there one time. And maybe Allison Channing, who works over at City Hall."

Was there a reason Lazelle was being so nebulous? I could flip a coin on that one.

"We are aware that a woman named Dixie Parks was a tarot client, and of course Brie Weatherby found the body," Mac added.

The server shook her head. "I don't know either of them."

"Do you have any idea who might have killed Mistress Quant?"

"Maybe somebody she went after on Instagram. Have you seen her channel? It's pretty good."

"What were you doing on Tuesday night?" I asked.

"Laundry."

"NOT EXACTLY A GREAT ALIBI," I told Mac on our way to the Macmobile after lunch. "And I guess the Wheel of Fortune card doesn't impress you much as a clue pointing to Jade Lazelle."

"Your conjecture is correct. At this point I find it nothing more than an interesting coincidence that Ms. Lazelle mentioned one of the tarot cards that lay on the table where Ms. Quant died. Nor is there any obvious motive for her."

"Not yet."

"Indeed."

"But she seemed nice."

NEXT UP WAS DIXIE PARKS, executive assistant to Arthur Vance Roeder, general manager of the Winfield Hotel at the corner of Market and Main, not far from Bobbie McGee's. I admit to a prejudice against people with three names, like John Wilkes Booth and Lee Harvey Oswald, but I learned that he went by just "Vance" in daily life. Roeder was married to old money—specifically Ellie Winfield Roeder, who owned the namesake hotel. Their daughter, Sandy, had been a student of Mac's. A smartly dressed woman in her mid-forties with well-coiffed auburn hair and flawless makeup, Parks sat at a desk outside Roeder's office. We'd called ahead and she was expecting us.

"Let's grab a coffee," she told us, standing up and taking her purse from the back of a chair. "Mr. Roeder said it would be okay. He's a wonderful boss. And so involved in civic activities. He's even president of the Erin Municipal Airport Board!"

I didn't even know there was an airport board until Johanna wrote a story about some controversy involving it, the details of which didn't stick with me.

"How noble," Mac praised.

"Mr. Roeder says anything that's good for Erin is good for the hotel."

The speed at which Dixie Parks walked and talked made me think she was in no great need of an afternoon caffeine hit. Nevertheless, she ordered a double espresso at Malarky's Pub on the first floor of the hotel as soon as the server rushed over to us.

"So, about Zoraida Quant," she said. "I was shocked, of course. I've never known anybody who was murdered. And so violently!"

Gripping his own mug of Columbian dark roast, Mac detoured around that whole murder thing and began on a more personal level:

"I gather that Ms. Quant read your future through tarot cards?"

"Right. Right. Well, she did the tarot thing for me. Whether I really believed in it, I'm not sure. But I believed in her."

The McCabe eyebrows, both of them, hiked up at that.

"What I mean is," Parks hurried on, "she gave me wise advice, wisdom I needed to hear, even though she was kind of blunt." *That's one word for it.* "Where that wisdom ultimately came from was less important to me. The first time I went to her it was on a spur of the moment because I was in a dark place. She turned over the death card"—*that again!*—"and when she told me my marriage was dead, I knew she was right. She gave me the courage to walk out on Luke Parks, who was a serial cheater almost the entire eleven years we were married. Actually, we're still married, but the divorce will be final soon."

Luke Parks? Where had I heard that name before?

"Not right after the first session, of course," Parks clarified. "At first, I resisted what she told me, but I began to see the wisdom of it, and I kept coming back. I could tell her anything. And I did." She chugged java. "I miss her already."

Lazelle and Parks had certainly dished up a different view of Zoraida Quant than I'd had before. The late witch seemed to be kind of a wisdom figure, wisdom sometimes being what a person needs to hear and not necessarily what she wants to hear.

"Mistress Quant wasn't exactly peaches and cream on her Instagram channel or in her antics when she was running for city council," I noted.

"People are complex," Parks said.

"Quite so," Mac intoned. "It is not uncommon for two individuals to describe a third person in completely different terms, and yet both may be accurate in describing the version of the person that each knew." He changed gears. "Did you see or hear anything at Witch's Brew that, in light of the murder, might indicate why someone would want to remove her from this life?"

After a moment's thought, Parks said, "Not that, but she made a lot of enemies with her Instagram channel—including Brie Weatherby, the woman who found the body."

Incoming! This was hot news!

"You know her?" Mac asked.

"Yeah. We were in an aerobics class together once. I saw her not long ago and she was very upset about Mistress Quant's social media posts."

"AND WEATHERBY DOES have a history of direct action," I reminded Mac.

"Throwing soup at a painting and bludgeoning a woman to death are hardly in the same genre, old boy."

"Still. And Dixie Parks seems like a reliable witness with a solid alibi."

Parks told us she'd been with friends at a performance of *The Music Man* (my favorite musical) at the SBU theater department's Davenport-Lattimore Bijou Theatre, preceded by an early dinner at Gatsby's. (Spoiler alert: That checked out.)

Brie Weatherby lived in a mid-century modern house, all steel and glass and flat lines, which told me she had some bucks. Dressed in pedal pushers and a sleeveless blouse that emphasized an admirable figure, she also had several arm and calf tattoos which didn't show up on TV during her interview with Bennington Lee. I liked the one of Betty Boop best. Another tattoo had scales, and I was glad to see that they were balanced.

"My boyfriend moved out last week, but he left behind some bad energy that's been blocking my creativity," Weatherby explained. "That's what took me to Mistress Quant's on Tuesday morning." This came after she got us seated in matching orange fiberglass Herman Miller chairs (current value $1,800 to $7,000, if produced in the 1950s) and offering us herbal tea, which we declined. She had all my McCabe & Cody books on the shelves behind her living room sofa and told us that she'd been expecting us. I was finding it hard not to like this woman, but I tried to keep my objectivity as the conversation moved along.

"Finding the body of the deceased must have been traumatic," Mac said.

Unless you made the body deceased.

She sipped her chamomile, then said, "We are all only temporary residents of our bodies."

"That is indisputable. Not all of us exit them through extreme violence, however. How long had you been getting readings from Mistress Quant?"

"I'd been visiting her every few weeks since earlier this year, whenever I was at a crossroads and felt I needed some direction or clarification. But I knew she also did house cleansings, and when I found myself in the neighborhood of Witch's Brew on Tuesday morning, I realized that's what I needed."

"What were you doing on Mulberry Street?" I asked, just to see if she had to think up an answer. But she responded quickly.

"I was at the library. I still like real books."

"In that I share your taste," Mac assured her. "With the benefit of hindsight, did you observe anything in your previous dealings with Mistress Quant that might be relevant to her murder—an argument with someone, for example?"

Weatherby stared out the huge window at the woods, probably her property, either trying to remember or calculating her reply. It struck me that she was well-toned and remarkably free of wrinkles for a woman heading toward 80 years old. Like the house, that must have cost a lot. We later found out that she was divorced from one Jason Weatherby, not from Erin, who was some kind of software legend that I'd never heard of.

"No, I don't remember anything like that," she said finally. "Of course, she did our readings in the evening, one on one, so we were alone then. I stopped in the shop a few other times, but not often."

I cut to the chase. "Isn't it true that you were very upset about some of her Instagram videos?"

"Where did you hear that?" she asked.

"That doesn't matter, if it's true," I parried.

Weatherby set down the tea. "It's true. I didn't like her smarmy attitude on the channel, and I felt like I'd paid her enough for her services to not be shy about telling her so. And some of her targets are friends of mine—Mallory Ziv in particular."

County auditor Ziv was not much younger than Weatherby, but unlike her had suspiciously dark hair. Whenever I saw Ziv on the news, I thought she looked like somebody who would hit you with a rolling pin if you didn't toe the line. I've voted for her four times so far.

"You seem to have a penchant for direct action when things upset you, as in your escapade at the Shinkle." I was on a roll. "Didn't you throw tomato soup at a Farny painting?"

"No, it was pea soup, my own recipe, and a Duveneck painting which was safely under glass. Nobody and nothing got hurt, Cody. The art was well protected, or I wouldn't have done it. And the front-page coverage in the local press called attention to the existential crisis our environment is facing. You know, McCabe, I wouldn't have let you in here if I weren't curious about how you would beard me in my den, as it were, having read about your previous escapades. Now that I know, I think you'd better go."

I was a little offended that she directed her ire at Mac. I was the one who brought up the soup slinging!

Not dallying, Mac stood. But he didn't go quietly. "Might I ask where you were on the night of the murder, Ms. Weatherby?"

"You just did. And I was with a certain gentleman friend who shall not be named. A lady never tells."

Apparently, the bad vibes left behind by the previous boyfriend hadn't sapped *all* of her energy.

Chapter Twelve
Might as Well Be Dead

"DO YOU THINK SHE'S a good suspect?" I asked Mac.

"No. Perhaps that is why we should suspect her."

And I suspected that he was just being elliptical for fun.

"Quant attacking her gal pal on an Instagram channel seems a poor motive for murder," I said. "But then, Ms. Weatherby clearly isn't your average bear."

"I would have put it differently, but your sentiment is sound. She rows her own boat, as it were, and making waves is her intention rather than a side effect. Apart from that, you undoubtedly observed the significance of one of her tattoos."

Undoubtedly.

"Sure, but maybe you could remind me."

"The scales on her forearm are a symbol of justice, and Justice is one of the tarot cards that could be a dying message. In Ms. Weatherby's case, it most likely represents her sign of the zodiac—Libra, the scales, which is your birth sign as well, Jefferson, your birthday being September 26."

I was pushing 50—hard—and didn't welcome that gentle reminder.

"Right," I said. "Sure. Well, that makes two suspects, if they are suspects, with connections to one of those cards."

"BRIE WEATHERBY HAS NO verifiable alibi and a tattoo that could link her to one of the tarot cards," Mac summarized to Oscar when we dropped by Court Street to debrief him. "Although you should check to see if any of the other suspects is a Libra, and therefore could have been indicated by the Justice card."

"I resent that," I put in.

"However, as Jefferson has observed, Ms. Weatherby has no very convincing motive, given that some negative comments about a friend on a poorly viewed Instagram channel do not meet that bar.

"Moving on, Jade Lazelle says that she was doing laundry on the night of the murder, which is no alibi, and also has a remote connection to one of the tarot cards, the Wheel of Fortune that she told us Ms. Quant turned over for her during a reading. However, not only does she have no known motive, she also seemed genuinely upset about Ms. Quant's murder and eager for the culprit to be found."

Oscar looked dazed by all the data, but we were just getting started.

"And then there's Dixie Parks," I said. "She also has no known motive, and no obvious connection to one of the tarot cards." Mac and I had talked that through. "In a change of pace, she does have an alibi—she was with a group of friends at *The Music Man* that evening, with dinner beforehand. It doesn't seem likely that the killer would have found Quant still in the shop after the play ended at almost tenthirty."

"Of course, the killer could have lured her to the shop," Mac noted, "although I do not find that highly plausible."

Plausibility is not the hallmark of your Damon Devlin mysteries, Mac.

"Quant's cell doesn't show a message from anybody asking to meet her that night," Oscar reported. "Oh, that reminds me. Arly called to tell me unofficially that the time of death is just what we expected—sometime Tuesday evening, not afternoon and not the next morning." He turned around to refuel from the Keurig. "And the blood on the murder rock was O negative, which is Quant's blood type. No fingerprints retrievable from said rock. No surprise there. Back to suspects: Gibbons doesn't think much of that Reverend Sapp or Quant's son in that regard, either. Their alibis checked out. So, there we are. When all else fails, don't overlook the obvious. Some friend or lover of Troy Braggs, probably Robin Hauser—"

"Sorry to interrupt, Chief." Holly Burdette stood in the doorway, not looking particularly sorry. "James Bridges is on line 6. He says it's about the Quant murder case."

"Okay, thanks." To us he said, "What the hell!"

James Hancock Bridges, of the Bridges Law Firm, is the bluest of blue-blood lawyers in Erin, with a silk-stocking clientele and no expertise in murder cases. A likable chap, he has that easy manner that often comes with old money, honed over years of sitting on every volunteer board in town. Oscar put him on the speakerphone. After the routine pleasantries, Bridges said:

"I'm calling as a good citizen, not as a lawyer. For many years our firm has represented members of the Applewhite family, including the late Zoraida Applewhite Quant." He didn't sound especially happy about saying her name. "Today I received a phone call from Russell Quant, her husband, who wanted me to know that he is alive and just arrived in Erin to visit his children. He saw the report about his wife's murder on PNN."

"The Quants never divorced?" Oscar said, just to be sure.

"They did not, at our client's insistence," Bridges acknowledged, "although there was a clear case of desertion involved."

"Therefore, under Ohio law, he has the right to half of Ms. Quant's estate even though he was not mentioned in her will," Mac said.

"That did not escape Mr. Quant's notice, which is why he called me." Jim Bridges's tone was ironic, dry as a martini made with no vermouth.

Oscar knew a hot new suspect when he heard about one. "Do you have his phone number?"

"Of course, and I don't mind sharing it with you. But if you should want to drop in on him unexpectedly, he's staying at Motel Sex."

That's not a typo; it's the nickname for a certain low-cost, poorly maintained motel just outside Erin city limits that is rumored to rent by the hour although unsuspecting travelers had been known to book in through the night. There wasn't a chance in 10 million that Bridges had ever been closer to the place than the sign observable from U.S. 52.

"Lynda's theory could be right," I said after Bridges disconnected.

Oscar gave me the hairy eyeball, so I had to explain my beloved's idea that Quant might be the killer, which I hadn't shared with him previously.

"What do you think of that?" the Chief asked Mac.

"When Jefferson originally shared Lynda's speculation about Mr. Quant as the killer, I dismissed it for lack of motive because I believed that the Quants were divorced. The fact that Russell Quant inherits half of what is apparently a rather large estate obviously changes the situation entirely."

"Worth a visit to Mr. Quant, anyway," the Chief said. "And I think I'll go on this one. Nice to get out of the office once in a while. Let's not call ahead—everybody likes surprises. But I still think the witch's demise was to shut her up. By the way, the judge granted Slade a continuance on the Braggs trial until we can figure out what's what."

"And who's behind it," I added.

I'D NEVER BEEN TO that motel—honest!—and I don't expect to make a return visit anytime soon. Let's just say it was no Winfield or Harridan Hotel, although it was probably a perfectly respectable place when it was built long before the advent of the interstate highway system. Oscar flashed his badge at the mousy desk clerk, producing a look of horror which dissipated when the poor man found out that all the Chief wanted was to speak to one of his guests.

As soon as Russell Quant opened the door, I think we all knew it would be a short visit. Quant sat in a wheelchair and breathed with the aid of a portable oxygen tank.

"I am sorry to see the condition you are in," Mac told him after the Chief had introduced us and explained why we'd knocked.

Quant was in his seventies, or at least looked it, with unkempt grey hair and deeply wrinkled skin.

"Thanks for the thought, but save your pity for somebody who deserves it," he said. "I did this to myself. At my peak, I smoked five packs of cigs and drank a bottle of Jim Beam a day, not to mention dabbling in what are technically known as controlled substances. I was well on my way to being the mess you see now before the car wreck that put me in a wheelchair. That's why Zory kicked me out all those years ago—all my bad habits adding up to the worst husband ever."

Mac raised an eyebrow. "You did not leave her?"

"Why the hell would I do that?"

Well, she had a few eccentricities of her own.

"Your children for many years have believed that you deserted them. And before that, they were under the impression that you were dead. Why did you never contact them?"

"Zory said she would cut me off if I did that."

"I assume you mean from bare subsistence financial support, not from sexual congress."

Quant just stared at Mac. So did I.

"How long have you been in town?" Oscar asked Quant.

"Just checked in a few hours ago."

Of course, he could have been in a nearby town and commuted to the murder. That happened in one of our other cases. And judging by his choice of hostelry, it wouldn't have bothered him much to stay at another cheap motel and pay with cash so as to not leave a trace.

"I called Zoe and Zane as soon as I got here," Quant added. "I've been keeping tabs on them from a distance, off and on, without them knowing. So, I had contact numbers for them. But they wouldn't even talk to me. It's like I'm dead to them. And I might as well be dead, just like poor Zory."

Chapter Thirteen
Witch TV

"ON THE FACE OF IT, it sure doesn't seem like Quant would have the strength to smash his wife's head 'with great force,' as I think Arly put it," Oscar said as we headed away from the sleazy motel towards his cruiser. "Also, it's hard to see him sitting in a wheelchair behind her, where Arly said the killer was when he struck, and then standing up to brain her on the top of her head."

"The wheelchair could be a blind to make us think just that," I pointed out. "Quant may be able to walk as well as any of us."

"Did you not notice his legs?" Mac asked, which was a rhetorical question if I ever heard one. "They did not come close to filling out his pants, which indicates to me that they were withered from lack of use."

"He could have hired a hit man."

"If he could afford that, he wouldn't be staying at Motel Sex," said Oscar, by this time behind the wheel.

"Maybe he can only afford that dump because he spent it on a hit man!" I thought that was pretty good. "Or maybe the hit man worked on spec, getting paid when Quant gets his inheritance. It wouldn't be the first time."

"Also, who ever heard of a hit man using a rock?" Oscar added.

"Nobody," I conceded. "But maybe dozens of hit men have used rocks, and they were never caught because they used rocks." I was on fire!

"Bravo, Jefferson!" Mac boomed.

"You think I'm right?"

"Not remotely. Not if you seriously posit Russell Quant as a good suspect. While not beyond the realm of possibility that Mr. Quant suddenly took it into his head to kill his wife after living on her largesse for decades, it does seem unlikely. A look at her more recent activities might be a more fruitful course of inquiry."

"Like for instance, planning to testify in court against Braggs, which probably caused Hauser to kill her, even though I can't prove it yet," Oscar said.

"Don't overlook Zane and Zoe Quant," I put in. "Apparently not knowing that their father would get half of Zoraida's estate, they would expect to split it 50-50. And according to Zoe, there was a lot to split. Maybe one or both of the siblings transitioned Mom into whatever comes next, as Zoe might say."

"You discount their alibis?" Mac asked.

"They're at least worth looking into."

"We did." Oscar tried not to sound smug, but it didn't work. "The Crawford family confirmed that Zoe was with them at Melinda's bedside doing her 'death doula' thing when Melinda breathed her last and for several hours after, while Zane's teacher friends remember him being around for several rounds of drinks and not too free with his pocketbook. The Crawfords highly recommended Zoe's services, by the way."

"Good to know," I said.

"'TODAY WILL MARK A major turning point if you channel your energies properly,'" Lynda informed me Friday during the morning chaos that is breakfast time for five at the Cody abode. "'Don't let the negativities of the past stop you from seizing your future. This is not the time to hold back. Be bold!'"

Reading my horoscope aloud to me is one of her morning rituals, along with completing the *Wall Street Journal* crossword puzzle.

"Maybe this means you should assert yourself with Mac on that witch business, darling," she added. She seemed to be dealing well with the collapse of her Russell Quant-as-Killer theory. And rightly so! Even Mac isn't right all the time, as this volume makes painfully clear. Besides, Lynda Teal Cody solved a mystery once and I'm sure she could do it again.[12]

"No doubt," I said. "On the other hand, I wonder what that horoscope would mean to Brie Weatherby if she really is a Libra like me. She doesn't seem like a woman who has to be told to be bold."

"Maybe it's a romance thing. Didn't you say she has a secret gentleman friend? Donata, quit pouting, it will give you wrinkles. Jake, finish your oatmeal. Sam, you may be excused."

This reference to Brie Weatherby and her love life somehow made me think I should be thinking of something,

---

[12] Yes! See my "Adventure of the Vatican Cameos" in *The Disappearance of Mr. James Phillimore* (MX Publishing, 2013) and *The Puzzle of the Purple Beret* later in this book. —L.T.C.

but the something was out of reach. I turned my attention to the obituary page. A brief notice informed me Zoraida Quant had been cremated and her ashes spread, appropriately, in Ramsey Park. "Services private."

MY MORNING COFFEE RITUAL at the office with Popcorn was cut short by a call from Lesley Saylor-Mackie telling me that one of our hallowed professors had been accused of plagiarism.

This was a hot-button issue at the time, of course, given similar charges popping up in Ivy League schools. In a surprise, the charge wasn't true. The accuser was a failed grad student out for revenge who claimed to see a connection between the professor's most recent work and an unpublished paper of his. But the course of action—as detailed in my frequently updated crisis communications plan—was exactly as if it had been true. We would be as transparent as possible, which meant revealing the names of both Dr. Elspeth Armstrong and her former student. GK, as president, was fully informed about the situation, and would be kept so by Saylor-Mackie. He liked to keep chain of command where possible, though trips upstairs to his office were not a rarity for me.

All this put me in the proper frame of mind for watching the deception, shenanigans, and hijinks of Zoraida Quant on her Instagram channel, "WitchCrafty," in midmorning after I finished my office chores. It was past time for me to catch up with Mac on seeing what Quant said about several citizens who had to be considered suspects in her murder, even if weak ones. Popcorn watched with me, insisting that it was part of her job description to assist me in all matters. Sparing you pain, I'll only hit some of the lowlights.

To take on Reverend Mayor Fred Sutterlee, Quant invaded services at his Apostolic Holiness Church of the Holy Spirit. The video started with congregants being slain in the spirit—falling on the floor while in religious ecstasy.

"I kind of wish city council members would do that," she told the viewers, standing outside the limestone church that had been built as a synagogue in 1927. "And I also wish a man of the cloth would stay out of politics."

Then came video of the mayor, who obviously never missed a meal, speaking in his familiar sonorous tones directly to the camera: "The Lord God works through human beings, and always has. And the civil order of our great nation is a mechanism for his servants to protect the vulnerable and when necessary, chastise the powerful."

"Remind me how much you get paid for being mayor?" came Quant's voice off camera.

"Approximately forty-two thousand dollars a year."

"Not bad for one council meeting a week." Here appeared video, without sound, of the mayor at a council meeting while Quant stood at the microphone during public comment time.

"There's a lot more to being mayor than the council meetings!" Popcorn fumed. "We know that from when Saylor-Mackie had the job."

"And he's too humble to say this, but his salary lets him serve the church without taking a penny from the congregation," I said. "So, it's not like he's rolling in dough." I briefly wondered if Reverend Adam Sapp took a church salary from his presumably smaller flock but decided that was irrelevant.

"So, if our mayor won't separate church and state, it's up to us to do it in the next election, fellow Erinites," Quant concluded after a little more bloviating.

"Mac would call that whole video 'bovine excrement,'" Popcorn said, accurately.

Next up on our playlist of Quant's hitlist was a double bill of Ralph Pendergast and Carson Kincade for their failed Underground Railroad Festival the previous autumn.

Ralph, a thin-lipped specimen with slicked-back receding hair and rimless glasses, is president of the Sussex County Convention & Visitors Bureau. An economist by training, in a previous life he was provost and academic vice president at what was then St. Benignus College—and a major pain in the posteriors for Mac and me. Quant and her camera caught up to Ralph as he was leaving his office. He did a fair job of not looking discombobulated.

"As head of the sponsoring organization, aren't you ashamed of your failed Underground Railroad Festival that was such a flop?" Quant asked him. Then came images of posters advertising the event. I don't know whether she put these videos together on her own or had help, but I'd seen a lot worse. Not as good as what Riley St. James turns out for SBU in our shop, but also not cringeworthy.

"Failed is a subjective term," Ralph said, and stopped there. *Not a bad response!*

"What I mean is, nobody came."

Video: Empty streets, which may or may not have been during the festival.

Ralph again: "Hundreds came." He didn't appear to be sweating.

"That's practically nobody. And worse, the whole idea exhibited a savior mentality, as if enslaved people needed white folk to rescue them."

At that point Ralph looked like he'd eaten a particularly sour lemon, then his image disappeared, to be replaced by a handsome, broad face with graying hair and blue eyes. He looked like a man whose tie was always straight even when he wasn't wearing one.

"It's a matter of historic fact that residents of Erin concealed slaves in their homes after those individuals crossed the river from Kentucky to freedom," he said. "Both white people and black people were involved. I don't know what you mean by savior mentality, but the Underground Railroad here in Erin helped to rescue people from the degradation of slavery, and we're proud of that."

Then Quant talked directly to the camera. "That was Carson Kincade, the brainbox behind the failed festival, who doesn't have as much money as you think the Kincades do. He fancies himself a mogul, but he's really just a dabbler who spends more than he has."

Dabbler or not, I thought Kincade's rejoinder on the "white savior" attack was a good one and had the added virtue of being true.

We ignored the videos attacking Marvin Slade and Mallory Ziv, the county auditor, in favor of one aimed at Mistress Quant's former competition. In it, Quant stood outside the shuttered shop of Madam Lena on College Street. Madam Lena's Parlor closed during the COVID shutdowns of four years previously—*four years already!*—but the sign was still there: A large open hand with the words FORTUNE TELLER PAST-PRESENT-FUTURE on the palm and the details written on

the four fingers and thumb: **OPEN NOW, PALM READINGS, CRYS-
TAL BALL, TAROT CARDS, $5**. This was the Instagram posting
Bennington Lee had excerpted, wherein Quant called Madam
Lena "a fake, a phony, and a fraud."

"Talk about kicking somebody when they're down!"
Popcorn exclaimed. "The window of Madam Lena's shop
must have cobwebs in it, it's been vacant so long."

"Yeah, that does make you wonder why she bothered," I said. I made a mental note to raise the point with
Mac.

The late witch ended that particular video with the
line, "For the real thing, come see me at Witch's Brew on
Mulberry Street, Erin."

"Somebody did," Popcorn observed.

Chapter Fourteen
"WitchCrafty" Targets

"DO YOU SEE ANY connections between Quant's Instagram targets and the tarot cards?" I asked Mac on the phone after an interval in which I worked a bit more on that messy charge of plagiarism (which wasn't plagiarism).

"Only those that we noticed previously. For example, 'Justice' could be seen as pointing to Marvin Slade as prosecutor—and the Fool could as well, given the contempt Ms. Quant exhibited for him."

"Tempting, and you've hinted at that before, but it's a stretch."

"Indeed! As is 'Wheel of Fortune' possibly referring to Carson Kincade because he is from a fortunate family or to Jade Lazelle because Ms. Quant drew that card for her during a tarot reading session. And Oscar called about an hour ago to say that none of Ms. Quant's targets or other clients was born under the sign of Libra, September 23 to October 22, except the highly unlikely Ms. Ziv. As an abstract proposition, I would say the Lovers holds the most promise, although I have no idea to whom it might refer."

I was inspired to say, "Troy Braggs and Robin Hauser! Oscar would be totally down for that. At least Hauser has a better motive than anybody else we know of."

"Her motivation is not as strong as it appears on the surface," Mac countered. "Clearly, she was willing to lie to protect her paramour. Having already done that, why kill the witness that she contradicted? With little hard evidence and contradictory testimonies, it was quite likely that Troy Braggs would be acquitted. At any rate, I am sure that the Chief's officers are giving Ms. Hauser their full attention."

I shifted. "What about Russell Quant? Are you sure about those withered legs?"

"Ah! I forgot to mention that Colonel Gibbons was able to confirm Mr. Quant's condition with that individual's personal physician in Michigan, who was willing to speak *sub rosa*, despite the questionable medical ethics, rather than face the possibility of being subpoenaed to court at some future time to do so officially."

"So, what do we do now?"

"We poke and prod at other individuals who would have reason to take joy in Ms. Quant's demise—those who came under her attack, however remote a tarot card connection might seem."

WE STARTED WITH CARSON Kincade, who had a small and unimpressive office on Oak Street not far from the river. We called first and he agreed to meet us there.

"Pay attention to his personal assistant, if he has one," I advised Mac. "PAs know more about their bosses than their bosses know about themselves."

This is not the place to go down the rabbit hole of personal assistant vs. administrative assistant vs. executive assistant, but PA seemed right to me for a small operation like Kincade's. And he did have a PA, sitting at a desk in a small waiting area as we entered. I had the distinct impression she'd been scrolling social media before our arrival.

"He's expecting you, but he called to say he's running a little late," she told us. Her name was Lulu Thatcher, according to the sign on her desk, and she was about 22 years old with a slim figure and dark neck-length hair that she kept running her fingers through. Her nails were painted white and well taken care of.

After thanking her, Mac asked, "What exactly does Mr. Kincade do?"

Thatcher leaned forward conspiratorially. "Not very much, let me tell you. He plays a lot of golf and owns a little real estate. And he's out of town a lot—cruises."

"Must keep you busy," I quipped. That was irony, not sarcasm, in case you wondered.

She shrugged. "This is part-time to fill out my resume and make a few bucks until I get into business school at Ohio University. I also work at the YMCA."

"About Mr. Kincade," Mac began. But he was interrupted by the arrival of that gentleman. And gentleman he was, at least in terms of social grades.

"I'm sorry to keep you waiting," he told us. "I had a business appointment."

The look on Lulu Thatcher's rather attractive face screamed "golf course!" Kincade was dressed for it in what is often called a golf shirt, although some people might consider that "business casual." But he was well shaved, his hair tidy, and he didn't look casual.

He took us into his private office.

"I know you by reputation, of course," Kincade told Mac as we settled into chairs. "That's why I agreed to see you. You said on the phone you wanted talk to me about Zoraida

Quant. I was too curious to say no, but I have no idea how I can help you or the police. I only ever talked to the woman once."

"That cannot have been a pleasant experience," Mac said.

"No, it was not. But what the hell, anybody can create and post a video on Instagram, TikTok, YouTube, Snapchat, and whatever's new since we began this conversation. That Adam Sapp guy took on Quant in his own video. Between them they probably got a few thousand hits."

"How did you wind up being in charge of the Underground Railroad Festival?" I asked, throwing a softball.

"It was my idea, I'm not ashamed to say. When I took over as the volunteer chairman of the Convention & Visitors Bureau, I knew we had to come up with some new events to pump up the local economy. The Underground Railroad connection to Erin is strong, and it's always good to play on your strengths."

"Your initiative is commendable," Mac said, "The negative reaction must have disappointed you."

"The old hag—pardon me—the late Ms. Quant exaggerated the blowback. It amounted to a few activists posting on social media about 'white savior mentality,' which I'd never heard of until then. I doubt if that had much impact on the success of the festival, or lack thereof. I was disappointed in the turnout, but this was the first year. These things build over time."

"Nevertheless, Ms. Quant calling attention to this year's less-than-successful outcome cannot have put her on your list of most favorite people."

Kincade looked like he wanted to be back on the golf course. "Well, I wasn't exactly pulling for her to win the Ohio lottery, but I'm appalled by her murder." *Because it's bad for conventions and visitors.*

"If I were a police officer I would ask where you were the night of the murder."

"And if you were a police officer, I would answer. But I would rather not say."

Both of the McCabe eyebrows lifted at that coy response.

"I will be happy to convey that to Chief Hummel," Mac said.

Kincade's sigh was accompanied by an I'd-love-to-catch-you-in-a-dark-alley look. "I was gambling at the Forty Thieves Casino in Cincinnati, with fair success."

"Alone?"

"Yes, alone! I wasn't stepping out with somebody else's wife, if that's what you mean."

No, we were wondering whether somebody could verify your alibi.

"I find it curious that Mr. Kincade refuted an unmade accusation," Mac said as soon as we were out on the sidewalk again. "Perhaps this is a case of the guilty flee where no one pursueth."

"Or maybe he was telling the truth, and he just thinks you have an evil mind that would suspect that."

"Quite possibly so, old boy."

"If he bought gambling chips with a credit card—I think you can do that in Ohio—there would be a record of the transaction that would prove he was there, right?"

"Indeed. It would not establish how long he was there, however. He could have bought the chips to create an alibi and then pocketed them."

RALPH PENDERGAST USED TO be Sebastian McCabe's bête noire (Mac's term) when Ralph was our boss, but that ended almost a decade ago. The relationship has mellowed out considerably since then. We assembled with him in his conference room, where his willowy assistant, Mary Landfair, passed out cups of coffee. She knows us well enough to make mine decaf without asking, although she herself finds jolt-less brew pointless.

"I don't understand how I can help," Ralph said.

"Just routine," I assured him.

"But I only met that witch person once."

"An encounter which led to her blasting into the mediasphere a video quite critical of your Underground Railroad Festival efforts," Mac noted.

Ralph put up his hands in a don't-blame-me gesture. "The whole fiasco wasn't my idea. I expressed skepticism when Carson first touted it."

"How is it, then, that the festival proceeded?"

Ralph almost smiled. "Office politics is not confined to the academic world, McCabe. Carson is not a true mover and shaker, but he has friends who are."

"I assume that Ms. Quant's video was not well received in the business community."

"There was a lot of snickering directed our way, I must admit."

"Schadenfreude is also not confined to the academic world," Mac observed.

I cut to the chase: "You know Kincade and we don't, Ralph. Do you think he might have been enraged enough to bash Quant's head in, maybe a spur-of-the-moment thing?"

When he just happened to be carrying a rock.

That was, after all, the reason for our visit—to get Ralph's take on Kincade. It's not like we could imagine our old antagonist as a suspect in a homicide by rock (or stone). He'd be more likely to bore a victim to death.

"Carson as a killer? I don't find that credible in the least," Ralph said. His opinions are always firm and sometimes correct. "If you insist on playing detective, you should take a good look at that Weatherby woman who found the body."

Mac raised an eyebrow, probably more at Ralph suggesting a suspect than at whom he suggested. "How so?"

"She's a so-called 'activist.' I wouldn't put anything past that crowd."

"I DO NOT FIND Ralph's reason for focusing on Ms. Weatherby to be very convincing," Mac said after we'd finished our coffees and headed off.

"No, but there is something about Weatherby that's been nagging at me. I'll let you know when I figure it out."

"Please do."

I'll give you the CliffsNotes version of the interviews that followed, which all took place at the taxpayer-funded offices of the interviewees.

REVEREND FRED SUTTERLEE, Erin mayor: "I warned Ms. Quant in our few encounters that playing with dark forces was bound to have dark consequences. She was in my prayers. I am deeply sorrowful that she did not heed my warning, and forfeited both life and, possibly, soul—although our God is merciful, and I would not presume to know her eternal destination."

MALLORY ZIV, Sussex County auditor: "Felt threatened by her? You've got to be kidding! I am *so* used to personal attacks since the new property tax assessment went out. You should see my emails. I'm even mad at myself—my assessment went up, too! Quant should have considered herself lucky. The taxes on her house only went up seven percent because her end of town isn't trendy right now. The owner of that building on Mulberry Street where she had her shop got hit with a twelve percent increase. I looked up the numbers."

MARVIN SLADE, Sussex County prosecutor: "Zoraida Quant took a cheap shot at me on her Instagram channel, but I'm the last person on earth who would want her dead. Without her, my case against Troy Braggs is down the toilet. I think Oscar's on the right path focusing on Robin Hauser—and I look forward to prosecuting her for Quant's murder. You can't seriously think anybody would kill the witch just because she went after them on social media?"

"I must concede it does seem unlikely," Mac told Slade. "There is, however, one Instagram target who was also a business rival of sorts, and that sort of competition has provoked more than a few murders. I refer to the palm reader Madam Lena, who is no longer in business. That is most likely not her real name, but her former landlord can tell us who she is."

"Good luck, McCabe. Hummel and Gibbons seem to be getting nowhere fast on this one."

And that is where this chapter would have ended if I hadn't gotten an inspiration that night during dinner. While telling Lynda about Ralph's lame finger-pointing at Brie Weatherby, it suddenly hit me what had been at the back of my mind, trying to move to the front, ever since breakfast.

"Weatherby!" I set down my grilled cheese sandwich.

"What about her, darling?"

"She said she went to Quant for a house cleansing because her boyfriend moved out last week and left behind some bad energy."

"So?"

"What if the BF didn't really move out? What if Weatherby killed him and Quant knew it, meaning that she had to be removed?"

"How would Quant know it?"

"Maybe it was really some time earlier, not Wednesday morning, that Weatherby went to Quant for a 'house cleansing.' And maybe she thought the 'bad energy' came from a dead boyfriend in the basement. And maybe she made the mistake of sharing that little detail with Quant in an off moment and later regretted it."

Lynda wrinkled her eyebrows in thought. "Isn't that a lot of maybes?"

"Maybe. But if all of them are true, Quant could have been trying to leave a clue to Weatherby with the tarot card called the Lovers! Remember, Weatherby has no alibi for the evening of the murder except an unnamed and possibly nonexistent gentleman friend."

Chapter Fifteen
Brie and Madam Lena

"BY THUNDER, JEFFERSON, you may be on to something!" was Mac's reaction when I delayed dessert to call him with my newborn theory. "Let us confront Ms. Weatherby tomorrow and get her reaction."

"Dragging the Chief out on a Saturday for that might be tough."

"And also premature, given the lack of evidence to back up your promising theory at this point. Let friend Oscar sleep in."

So, Saturday morning—when I would have liked to be giving my Schwinn a workout along the riverfront— found just the two of us back at Brie Weatherby's mid-century modern house. For some reason, she didn't seem happy to see us.

"What now, Holmes and Watson?" was her greeting as she flung open the door.

I am not Mac's—

"May we come in?" Mac asked, not at all nonplused by Weatherby's pink PJs and unkempt hair.

"Make it quick and painful."

Before Mac could say anything, I took her at her word and leveled both barrels:

"You killed the man who was living with you, which is why you had to have your house cleansed of his unquiet spirit, then killed Quant so she couldn't tell anyone."

Call it shock therapy. In response, Weatherby didn't offer us tea or tell us to sit down. She just stared at me for what seemed like eons, then at Mac, with her arms crossed over her ample bosom all the while.

"You are flipping crazy," she said finally. Except she didn't actually say "flipping."

"Is that a denial?" Mac asked.

"You're flipping right it is! Carl Petermann is the so-called man who shared my bed and board for most of this year until he decamped. And I doubt that's a secret, given Carl's blabber mouth. But you can ask him if you want, given that he's all-too-much alive, that waste of perfectly good DNA."

Carl Petermann! The mind boggled at the notion. I knew him as an employee of the main branch of the Public Library of Erin and Sussex County, which isn't far from Witch's Brew on Mulberry Street. But wait! Weatherby had said she was at that library when she got the idea of visiting Mistress Quant to ask for a home cleansing. Maybe seeing Carl set her off.

Balding with horn-rimmed glasses, Carl works the checkout desk, where I first observed the " tattooed in blue on his right wrist. He is also a charter member of the Lyceum Players amateur theater group, along with Mac, and performs amateur magic as the Great Carlini.[13] But he was apparently a better magician than I imagined if he managed to charm Brie

---

[13] See *The 1895 Murder* (MX Publishing, 2012) and *Murderers' Row* (MX Publishing, 2020.)

Weatherby. The Magician—one of the tarot cards! Although how or if that meant anything, I had no idea. Why would he want to kill Zoraida Quant? But in a world where Carl Petermann was some kind of dance-away lover, anything could happen.

Weatherby must have read the shock on our faces at Carl's name because she added by way of explanation, "I must admit he is very good at reading a girl poetry."

"May I ask the reason for his disaffection with you?" Mac inquired. To me, that was TMI—I mean, I wasn't sure I wanted to hear any details of a romance between those two strange ducks. But my brother-in-law is always curious, and Weatherby didn't seem to mind answering.

"Carl is a little old fashioned. It didn't sit well with him when he found out I was fooling around with somebody else on the side."

I would have fallen out of my chair if I'd been sitting in one.

But Mac merely arched an eyebrow. "The man you were with on the night of Ms. Quant's murder, perchance?"

"You're pretty fast on the uptake, McCabe, I have to admit."

"I think I can go even further, Ms. Weatherby. Since you exhibit no reluctance at all to discuss your cohabitation with Mr. Petermann, there must be some reason other than discretion that causes you to be so reticent about naming your other paramour. You do not seem unduly concerned about your own privacy; therefore, you must be protecting him from something. Perhaps he is married? No, not that. What then? Given your exploit at the Shinkle, and the inability of the museum to establish how you got past the guard with the soup, I submit that you initiated a romance with someone at the museum—most likely the guard himself—in order to facilitate your protest."

The expression on the activist's much-lifted face said that she was floored by this suggestion. But not because it was wrong.

"You no longer amuse me," she informed Mac after a pause. "You can go now."

"The level of cynicism involved in undertaking an *affaire de coeur* for that purpose is impressive," Mac added.

Weatherby gave a crooked smile. "It wasn't only that. The gentleman in question has other attributes, and I don't mean poetry-reading skills. Now get out."

"The Murdered Lover was an excellent theory," Mac said, back in the Macmobile. "It only suffered from the defect of being wrong."

Now I feel much better.

"How did you know she was fooling around with some guy at the Shinkle?"

"Strictly speaking, I did not know. I was employing the cold reading technique I have used as a conjurer, the same method often used by mediums and psychics. When I mentioned the possibility that the man with whom she dallied on the murder night—presuming such a person existed—was married, I could tell by the expression on her face that was not the situation. And then, of course, when I struck upon the truth with my second conjecture about the guard, she removed all doubt that I was correct by inviting us to leave."

"Oh."

"On to Madam Lena."

"What's the story there?" All I knew was that Mac had called Gulliver Mackie to find out Madam's real name. Gulliver, who is only incidentally my boss's husband, owned the building with the now-outdated palm sign out in front.

"Ah, there I have a surprise for you, old boy. With some reluctance, Gulliver revealed that Madam Lena is in fact a young woman named Alena Pendergast."

"Pendergast! You mean—"

"She is Ralph's niece."

I DON'T KNOW WHAT I expected a palm reader to look like, but Alena Pendergast, aka Madam Lena, wasn't that. She was a cute young woman with orange hair, early 30s at the oldest. Instead of the shawl I might have expected from a fortune teller, she was clad in jeans and a T-shirt with that signature Rolling Stones logo—big red lips with a tongue sticking out. Nothing about her reminded me of her Uncle Ralph. She lived on a houseboat on the Ohio River, which made me wonder whether the footwear she was wearing would be classed as trainers, sneakers, or deck shoes. I'm a word guy.

"My parents back in Huntington were always asking what I was going to do for a living with a degree in psychology," she told us as she cracked open a beer. "Turns out that was a really good question. I was a grad student at Licking Falls when I started investigating the psychology of fortune telling in all its various forms. That led to a whole new career I never foresaw."

Never foresaw? Some fortune teller you are!

"So, I moved here—away from my old professors, and on the river—and set up shop. There were some bumps along the way, but it worked out well in the end."

"Until, that is, Zoraida Quant launched an assault on your credibility," Mac said.

"What? Are you kidding? That was great publicity. There's nothing like a controversy to boost a business. That's psychology, too."

"You have a business?" I asked. "Your former shop on College Street was shuttered by COVID."

"Right. And it never reopened because I couldn't afford the rent due to lack of income for several months. But Mr. Mackie was nice enough to let me out of the lease. Overall, it was the best thing that could have happened to me." She indulged in a swallow of Cincinnati-brewed Flying Pig Porter. "I had to switch to a new business model. Now I do online aura readings, sell spells on Etsy, and appear at bachelorette parties throughout the tristate, which are a lot of fun. In fact, I have one tonight. I'm also selling my inventory from the old store online at better prices than I could get in Erin, and I have an income stream from my TikTok channel. The Madam Lena gig more than pays the rent and I do a little e-commerce in collectibles on the side."

"Impressive," Mac said. He must have been reading my mind. "You make a convincing case that you had no reason for animus against Ms. Quant," Mac said.

"Not hardly! Like I said, she gave me a publicity boost. Now all my student loans are paid off and I'm a happy camper. Hey, would you guys like your palms read?"

Chapter Sixteen
Motive

"WE DIDN'T HAVE TO get out of there so fast," I complained to Mac the next afternoon. "It might have been fun to have our palms read."

"What ineffable twaddle!"

We were in the Mac Cave, Mac's man cave that he likes to call his study. Granted, it has a desk, a love seat, some nice chairs, a fireplace, and thousands of books lining the walls, some of which he wrote. But it also has a bar with a flat-screen TV above. How many studies do you know of that have a bar?

Anyway, that's where we went while our spouses headed to the Cincinnati Zoo with the young Codys after Sunday Mass on that beautiful autumn day.

"Weatherby and Madam Lena both looked promising, except for that small matter of no convincing motive," I told Mac, although he knew that.

"Motive," he mused. "Except in the case of an individual moved to act by revenge or pure hatred, a killer expects to profit in some way from the victim's removal from the scene. What has changed now that Ms. Quant no longer walks among us?"

"Well, for one thing, that spooky old shop of hers will get a new tenant."

I thought I was just being flip, but Mac thumped his desktop, almost spilling the beer that resided in a glass there. "Hell and damnation, Jefferson! Perhaps that is it!"

"Oh, absolutely! No doubt! But . . . what exactly is what?"

"Real estate! Perhaps this is all about real estate. Am I correct in thinking that the area around Mistress Quant's Witch's Brew has undergone something of a revival, becoming rather chic and therefore rendering the properties more valuable?"

We were in my wheelhouse now. I learned about buying, selling, and renting property at my father's knee. He was one of the most successful Realtors in my hometown in Virginia.

"Your eyes don't lie," I assured Mac. "There are some tony new businesses there, including a dress shop that has seen entirely too much of the Cody credit card."

"That neighborhood rebirth would explain Ms. Ziv's reference to the higher increase in property taxes suffered by Ms. Quant's landlord compared to Ms. Quant herself," he said. "Said individual would greatly benefit by the Wiccan's demise, giving him or her the opportunity to rent the building to a much higher-end and higher-paying tenant after buying her heirs out of the lease. I wonder who that owner is."

By this time, Mac was already playing his fingers across the computer keyboard. "Ms. Ziv may not be the most charming public official in our acquaintance, but her county auditor's website is quite efficient for finding out who owns property. Ah ha! Ms. Quant's landlord was Carson Kincade."

This was hard to wrap my head around. "You really think he's Quant's killer?"

"I think it a compelling theory. Murder not out of pique at her unflattering Instagram post about him but murder for profit."

"And the tarot cards clue?"

"The Wheel of Fortune perhaps, although I do not insist upon it."

Mac picked up his cell phone.

"Who are you calling?"

"Oscar. And then Carson Kincade."

But Oscar refused to come out and play, citing lack of evidence against Kincade. (He didn't have any real evidence against Robin Hauser, either, which is why she wasn't in jail. But never mind that.) "Be sure and let me know if you get a confession," he added.

WE CAUGHT UP WITH Kincade on the 12th hole of the Erin Country Club, where he was playing a foursome with Winfield general manager Arthur Vance Roeder, *Observer* editor-at-large (in reality a columnist) Frank Woodford, and—Gulliver Mackie!

Golfing has always been big in the business world, and bigger than ever now, according to a *Wall Street Journal* story I'd read a few months earlier called "A Killer Golf Swing Is a Hot Job Skill Now." My bosses, GK and Lesley Saylor-Mackie, play golf on occasion with some of our donors and board members (not necessarily different categories). As for me, I know approximately as much about golf as I do about astrophysics.

Introductions of the foursome weren't necessary, and Kincade didn't offer any.

"What the hell is this all about?" he demanded. Even with a golf cap on his head and a club in his hand, he looked natty. But at the moment also angry. "I already talked to you about that crazy witch lady. Can't a man have a little peace even on the back nine?"

His trio of golfing buddies all looked like they wanted to say, "Yeah, what the hell!" But more than that, the expression on Frank Woodford's broad, black face telegraphed that he saw a doozy of a story here. These chronicles have frequently noted Frank's penchant for spending time on the links even when he held the title of editor and general manager of the *Observer*. But he picked up a lot of stories as well as a lot of advertising business that way.

"When we spoke earlier, I was unaware that you owned the building in which Ms. Quant's shop was located," Mac told Kincade.

"What does that have to do with anything?"

"I suggest that it may have everything to do with Ms. Quant's murder. Based on her character, I presume that she was a troublesome tenant and undoubtedly locked into a lease at a price far lower than could be commanded in today's market."

"Yeah, so?"

"If she were gone, you could buy her heirs out of the lease and then rent out the building for more or sell it at a far higher price than you paid eleven years ago."

Gulliver Mackie, whose photo should appear in the dictionary along with his spouse under the word "distinguished," looked like he wanted to say something but didn't. He probably does a lot of that as wealth manager for almost

all the big-money names in Sussex County and more than a
few in Cincinnati and Louisville. He also owns a sizable
chunk of downtown Erin (including, as previously noted,
Madam Lena's former digs).

Kincade was less reticent, though not very articulate:

"That's just . . . What you're implying . . . You are so
full of—" At that point, words failed him. Mac suffered no
such debility.

"Perhaps the tarot card Wheel of Fortune was meant
to refer to you as the offspring of a wealthy or perhaps once-
wealthy family," he said, "although that interpretation may be
confirmation bias on my part. What is more certain is that
you knew about Reverend Adam Sapp's reference to stoning
witches. You mentioned that in your earlier conversation
with us. Therefore, you were in a position to choose a stone
as the murder weapon so that it would point away from you
and toward a convenient suspect."

"I told him about Sapp's video on the fifth hole one
day," Vance Roeder put in. "You might as well accuse me."

Don't tempt us.

Roeder was in his late sixties, with round glasses and
suspiciously brown hair combed straight back. I'd seen him
around town, and I knew his daughter, Sandy.

I don't know what Mac would have said in response
because he didn't get the chance.

"You're over your skis this time, Mac," Gulliver
Mackie said, breaking his silence. "I've just been waiting to
hear you out. Everything you've said makes a sort of sense
except in the real world. The fact is, I'd already agreed last
month to buy the property you're talking about at a price that
reflects the value it will have when Ms. Quant's lease expires

in three months and a new tenant moves in—a jewelry store. Her death has no financial benefit for Carson."

Frank Woodford looked fascinated. But I didn't expect to see this written up in his "To Be Frank" column. One of Frank's hidden talents is discretion, which is why his dance card is always filled at the country club.

"IT COULD HAVE BEEN worse," I assured Mac on our way back to his car after he'd made a humiliating apology. (See online dictionary under "grovel.")

"Worse? I fail to see how."

"Oscar could have been here to witness that fiasco. He'd never let you forget it." *As if you could.*

Mac grunted.

"And he wasn't with us yesterday at Weatherby's, either. Look on the bright side—we're running out of people to falsely accuse."

Chapter Seventeen
One Less Suspect

IN LATE MORNING ON Monday, September 9, Arthur Vance Roeder called 911.

"My executive assistant didn't show up for work and isn't answering her cell," he said in a scared voice. A TV news report later used the 911 audio. "That's not like her. She's totally reliable. I'm worried that something might be wrong."

In what seemed to be a shock-induced moment of honesty, he later told Sebastian McCabe that although he deeply worried about her—"she was going through a tough divorce"—there was a selfish aspect to his anxiety as well. He was also aware that he couldn't function well in his Winfield job or his civic activities without Dixie Parks.

In a bigger city, say Columbus or Akron, such a call might have resulted in the 911 operator telling Roeder to chill out until she was missing for a couple of days. But this was Erin. Officer Fiona Bertsch went to Parks's house to check, fearing at worst that Mrs. Parks might have had some sudden illness that left her unconscious or delirious. Instead, she found the back door of the modest Cape Cod home broken open and inside a dead body with the head a bloody mess.

"ONE BULLET," ARLY EPPENSTEINER informed Mac and me. "Very efficient. Happened sometime last night. No gun in her hand, so not suicide—unless it was, and somebody wanted to make it look like it wasn't."

We'd been down that road before.

If Arly sounded cold, I've come to know her well enough to realize that's a defense mechanism against becoming too emotionally involved to do her job well.

Officer Bertsch, who is in her mid-twenties but looks younger and not especially cop-like, was still on the scene along with Oscar and L. Jack Gibbons at the time Mac and I arrived. The deceased, covered with a sheet, was being removed. I'd only met Dixie Parks once, but she'd been so vibrant that the sight of her still body filled me with a sadness that would be with me for days.

"The next-door neighbor, a Mrs. Schmidt, said she heard a loud noise that was probably the shot around seven-thirty," Gibbons told us. "Mrs. Schmidt's dog started barking, but she didn't think much of it. Assumed it was a car backfiring."

"Have you ever heard a car backfire?" I asked.

"No."

The living room, where the body was found, was in disarray, with a number of decorative tins opened as if someone had been looking for money within.

"Clearly not a robbery, despite a feeble attempt to make it seem as one," Mac said.

"How do you figure that?" Oscar asked. He was dressed for business with his chief's hat on instead of the Erin Eagles baseball cap he often wears.

"I figure that quite easily, Oscar, though in multiple ways. First of all, the lights in the house are on, despite the full sunshine at the moment, which means they were on when your forces arrived. You would not have turned them off until you had completed dusting the room for prints, a chore which is still in progress. I note that an automobile, presumably Mrs. Parks's, is parked at the back of the house where a burglar would have seen it. Lights on in the residence plus an auto in the driveway equals resident at home. No opportunistic burglar would have taken that as an invitation to break in. Nor do most burglars carry a gun."

"And, besides," I added, just to pound a nail into the coffin of the burglar theory, "there isn't a snowball's chance in hell you would have dragged Mac into this business if you thought it was a burglary gone wrong, and you wouldn't make a mistake about that."

"Ergo," Mac concluded, "it was not a burglary, despite the break-in to make it appear as one. Most likely Mrs. Parks admitted her killer, who broke in the back door on his or her way out."

"So, do you think this homicide is connected to the Quant case?" Bertsch asked. "I mean, I know the vic here was a client of the witch."

"Quite possibly," Mac allowed. "Perhaps even probably. However, I can think of four scenarios.

"Scenario One: The Quant and Parks murders are unrelated and the fact that the victims knew each other was mere coincidence, and coincidences do happen. The killer of Mrs. Parks could be her soon-to-be-ex-husband Luke Parks, for example."

"Wait a minute," I intervened. "We've had two cases in which there were two different murderers of connected victims. Wouldn't three be stretching credibility?"

"Only in fiction. In real life, not at all.

"Scenario Two: The two murders are related and have the same motive—someone killed both women for the same reason, a reason which I cannot perceive at this point but might eventually."

"Scenario Three: Mrs. Parks was that familiar woman in fiction: The Woman Who Knew Too Much. That is to say, she knew or could come to know who killed Ms. Quant."

"That's a cliché," Gibbons pointed out.

"So is a faked burglary," Bertsch riposted.

"So maybe Parks went to Quant's on the night of her murder—even though she wasn't on Quant's calendar with an appointment that night—and she saw Robin Hauser kill the witch," Oscar said.

"Scenario Four: None of the above," Mac barreled on.

"What the hell does that mean?"

"I have no idea, Oscar. However, not being omniscient, I have to allow the possibility that there is something I have overlooked."

Do you really believe any of that sentence?

Just then there was a commotion at the door. "Let me through!"

That was Vance Roeder, wearing a Brooks Brothers suit but looking totally unraveled.

"What happened?" he demanded. "I called Nine-One-One a couple of hours ago, but I couldn't just sit around knowing that Dixie might be hurt. What are all the cop cars doing here?"

By this time the EMTs, the coroner, and Dixie Parks were all gone.

"I'm afraid I have some bad news," Oscar said. "Mrs. Parks has been murdered."

"Murdered!"

He sat down in a chair, and if there hadn't been a chair there, I think Roeder would have gone down anyway. The shock seemed real to me, but what do I know about acting? And then I thought: *Is this the way a man reacts to news like that when his relationship with the dead woman is professional and personal but not romantic?* At that point Popcorn invaded my mind. I thought of all that Aneliese Pokorny and I had been through together over the years, and how important she was to me as my work spouse and as a friend, and how shattered I'd be if I lost her. And answered my own question with: *That's for damn sure how I'd react.*

"Do you know who did it?" Roeder asked Oscar in a tone of voice like freshly sharpened knives.

"Not yet, but we will."

"Look closely at her piece-of-shit husband, Luke. I wouldn't put it past him."

"Did she express fear of him?" Mac asked.

Roeder gave Mac a "you again!" kind of look, as if just realizing that he was there. "I'd say contempt more than fear. She didn't want to talk about her marriage mess, but I let her know that Ellie"—Arthur's wife, Ellie Winfield Roeder—"and I were there for her. She was planning to have a divorce party, and we were going to be there with bells on."

I'd read of this phenomenon, although I'd never heard of one in Erin. It seemed rather ghoulish to me, dancing on the grave of a marriage.

"We've called Mr. Parks to inform him of his wife's passing and will be having a little chat with him at the station," Oscar assured him. Oscar and his little chats!

Close to tears, Roeder talked on a little more, kind of babbling. That's when he confessed that self-interest was part of the reason he'd called 911—how much he depended on Dixie Parks in the office.

"Back to Robin Hauser," Oscar said after Roeder had departed, still looking shocked and devastated. "If she killed two women for Troy Braggs, I just don't get it. He's a scumbag."

"And there's another woman who's been visiting him in jail," Gibbons said. "Laurie Meeker, a nurse."

"Bad boy syndrome," Bertsch said with an air of wisdom.

Oscar's phone rang. "Hummel. Oh, joy. Tell him we have nothing to say yet. Thanks."

He hung up.

"That was Holly. Bennington Lee from PNN is back in town."

Chapter Eighteen
All Shook Up

"Mr. Roeder was right, you know," Mac said as we piled into his big red machine for the ride downtown to police headquarters. "An unfaithful husband is unreliable at best."

"And," I added, "a spouse is the most likely killer, statistically speaking, despite fancy theories." *In which we specialize.*

Roeder had told us that Luke Parks was a maintenance man at Altiora Corp. "when he's not performing as a low-rent Elvis impersonator." His day job at Altiora wasn't really a day job because he worked the night shift. Gibbons had awakened Parks to tell him of his wife's demise but offered no opinion as to the soon-to-be-ex's reaction to the news. If it really was news to him.

"It took him a while to process what I was saying," Gibbons had told us. "Or he was putting on a good act. I couldn't say which."

While Mac drove, and puffed on a cigar, I shoved all that to the back of my mind and worked my cell. It was another beautiful fall day, warm for September, and Mac had the Chevy's top down. After an exchange of affectionate texts with Lynda, the precise nature of which is none of your business, I had three media calls to return. Popcorn can't do everything for me while I play in Mac's sandbox. The most pressing of the trio one was from *Higher Ed Insider* about the plagiarism that wasn't. Not that SBU itself is important to that national publication, but *Insider* veteran J. Randolph Smith was working on a trend story. The hard part was saying something that was both true and didn't sound canned. I came up with:

"At St. Benignus University, we don't just have strong policies against plagiarism, Randy—we enforce them. But we're equally committed to the principle of 'innocent until proven guilty.' In the Tracy Foxe case, after a thorough investigation by a committee of specialists in the field, we were able to establish that . . ."

"AT 7:30?" LUKE PARKS repeated. "That's when Dixie was killed?" Apparently, Gibbons hadn't covered this in the phone call, or Parks hadn't processed it. Or door number three, he was yanking our chain, and he was lying when he said, "I was working my shift."

"Not on a break or at dinner at that particular time?" Oscar clarified.

"No. Both of those are later. You can check with my foreman."

We were back in Oscar's conference room. Parks was drinking coffee, and I couldn't help but think with sadness of Dixie and her double espresso the day Mac and I talked to her at the Winfield.

The sideburned Parks looked like young Elvis before he gained all that weight. Maybe it's just because of what I'd heard about him from his wife and from Roeder, but to me he gave off the vibe that everything about him was an imper-sonation of sorts—including the semblance of grief when he talked about Dixie. Also, he looked like he needed a cigarette from the package he had in his front shirt pocket.

"Some people would say you had good reason to kill your wife before the divorce was final," Oscar informed him. "This way you inherit at least half of her estate under Ohio law, no matter what her will says."

"Estate?" He made it sound like a foreign word. "You mean her money?"

"Money, stocks and bonds, property," Mac spelled it out.

The pseudo-Elvis shook his head mournfully. "Not much of that. We own a house, and we're current on our bills. That's about it. Dixie made good money, but I never saw much of it. She liked to shop."

It sounded almost like an accusation.

"Maybe it was her revenge for your infidelity," Mac said.

"Tomcatting around," I translated.

"I know what infidelity means," Parks snapped. "I admit I wasn't a good husband. I guess I just didn't get the one-woman gene."

Of all the pathetic excuses I'd ever heard that one de-served top billing.

"You were a patron of Long John Gold's Treasure Chest, a pawnshop," Mac noted. *Long John's!* Now I remem-bered—Parks's name was on that list of customers that Long John gave us when we were poking into the robbery. I felt a little irked that Mac hadn't reminded me of that. But then, he probably thought I remembered. The name Parks had sounded vaguely familiar to me when it first came up attached to Dixie as a Quant client, and Luke Parks even more so when Dixie had mentioned her unmentionable spouse, but the connection to Long John had eluded me.

"I had a little cash crisis, nothing big, so I pawned one of my guitars for a few days."

"What's with the Elvis gig?" Oscar asked. I assumed this was a technique—throw an unrelated question at the suspect to catch him off balance. Or maybe Oscar just wanted to know about the Elvis gig.

Some people might say Parks smiled at the question, but I say he smirked.

"It's a weekend thing," he said. "The women love it. That's what got me into trouble with Dixie—especially the bachelorette parties. They can get a little wild, one thing leads to another. I also do bar mitzvahs and retirements."

Good to know.

It struck me that Parks's infidelity probably had more to do with his jeans than his genes. I also wondered briefly whether Elvis and Madam Lena ever crossed paths at bachelorette soirees.

"Of course, the house will be full of your fingerprints, so that is no help in establishing whether you entered it with fatal intent," Mac mused.

"I couldn't do that even if I wanted to," Parks said. "Dixie changed the locks on me after she kicked me out three months ago. Apparently, I sent a sext message to the wrong woman. I came home one morning and found all my stuff on the porch."

"Even the guitars?" I asked.

He looked grim. "Both of them. Good thing it didn't rain."

"Mrs. Parks could have let you in last night," Mac pointed out.

"Could have, but wouldn't have," Parks pushed back. "She wouldn't even communicate with me except through her lawyer, Sally Fair."

As a young associate at SladeLaw, Erica's firm, Sally handles mostly civil work, although she also dabbles on the criminal side.

"We'll be talking to Ms. Fair," Oscar assured him. "Do you have any idea who killed your wife?"

"No way, no how! I just can't believe this happened." Parks actually teared up and there was a catch in his throat when he said: "Dixie was the sweetest woman on God's green earth. She really didn't deserve me." *How true!* "I was happy for her when she told me she moved on."

Mac raised an eyebrow. "You mean—"

"I mean she had herself a boyfriend."

"Who?" Mac and Oscar asked at the same time.

He shrugged. "I tried to wheedle that out of her, but she wouldn't give."

Then Luke Parks started crying.

Chapter Nineteen
Public Business

"WHAT DID YOU GET out of all that?" Oscar asked when Parks had slunk away.

"His tears are for himself," Mac said. "He feels guilty, and rightly so, though not of murder."

"What about Dixie's new squeeze? That sounds promising."

"Maybe it was Roeder," I said. "That would explain his eagerness to point the finger at Elvis. I had his relationship with Dixie pegged as office spouse, but maybe it turned into something else. And that wouldn't have been a good career move for Roeder, given that his wife owns the hotel he manages."

Before Mac could praise the brilliance of that observation, we heard, "Hi, guys!"

It was Tall Rawls striding into Oscar's domain like she owned the place and fairly glowing with cheerfulness.

"You're late," I chided. "We missed you at the murder scene."

I swear she blushed. "I was with Seth."

"Congratulations, Johanna!" Mac boomed. "May your wedded bliss be always blissful."

"How did you know?"

"I observed the fourth finger of your left hand."

It was newly decorated with a diamond ring.

"You're engaged!" No flies on me.

I hugged her, then Mac and Oscar did likewise. Police chiefs don't normally hug police reporters, but this was Erin.

"Lynda will be so happy," I told her. "How did you get Seth to commit?" I certainly couldn't claim credit, given that my intention to "give that boy a talking-to" came to naught when Seth instead dragged me into the problem of his stolen e-bike.

Johanna gave my question an enigmatic smile and a coy, "Details will not be provided."

Maybe an ultimatum was involved, something along the lines of "I get a ring, or we are no longer a thing." But that didn't seem like Johanna's style. Maybe Seth just wised up and got down on his knees and proposed. He wouldn't have far to go, given his height.

"I can recommend an Elvis impersonator and a palm reader for your bachelorette party," I told the newly affianced (Mac's word).

"Anyway," Johanna continued, giving my quip all the attention it deserved, "being otherwise occupied, I didn't hear about Dixie Parks on the scanner, which is why I didn't make it to the crime scene. But I got a tip." Probably from Holly, but Oscar let that slide. "At least Bennington Lee's not here."

Yep, Holly was her source. She would have told Johanna that Oscar gave Lee the brush-off. At one time Johanna seemed to regard the cable news veteran as an aspirational figure, but now he was competition.

"So, update me, Chief," she concluded, notebook in hand.

Oscar did so—the 911 call, Bertsch finding the body, the back door broken open, the shot heard by the neighbor, all that.

"What aren't you telling me?" she asked at the end.

Excellent question!

"I've given you all the facts," Oscar said piously. "Anything else would be speculation, and it's too early to speculate."

Johanna turned to Mac and said, "If you're here, you're helping Chief Hummel." Two minutes ago, everybody was hugging; now Johanna was a reporter, and Oscar was Chief Hummel. Lynda would be proud (of Johanna, not Oscar). "And you wouldn't be helping the Chief with a simple burglary gone wrong. So, what's up, Mac?"

"Perhaps I am just here for a social visit with a friend."

In full journalist mode, Johanna snorted and tried again with a more specific question. "Is there any connection between Ms. Parks and the recently murdered Zoraida Quant?" The question seemed aimed at anybody willing to answer. That sure wasn't going to be me.

Oscar looked at Mac, who looked at Oscar. I'm pretty sure the unspoken dialog was along the lines of, "Why not?" Then Oscar slowly pulled the curtain away from the tarot angle that he and Mac had been holding back.

"Parks was a client of Quant," he began.

"Client? You mean customer?"

"I don't mean she shopped in the store. Quant gave tarot readings—that thing where those goofy cards are supposed to predict the future, but don't quote me on that. Parks was one of the people she did it for, by appointment outside of regular shop hours."

"And she was killed at her shop outside of regular hours. So, do you think her murder and that of Ms. Parks are related?"

"That would be speculation . . ."

"And it's too early to speculate. Right." Knowing a dead-end when she saw one, Johanna tried another road.

"What do you know about Dixie Parks?"

"She was going through a divorce, had no children, and worked as the executive assistant to Arthur Vance Roeder, general manager of the Winfield Hotel."

"What do you know about Mr. Roeder?" Mac asked Johanna.

Being a reporter, and a good one, she unloaded.

"I've written a little about him. His wife owns the hotel, of course; I'm sure you know that. So, she's old money, but he's not. I kind of assumed at first that the job came with the marriage, but it was the other way around. Roeder came here from Pittsburgh in the 1980s with a degree in hotel management and worked his way up the ranks. I'm sure that marrying Ellie Winfield at the time her father both owned and managed the hotel didn't hurt. That was about 35 years ago, if I remember right. But I get the impression Roeder's also good at what he does, well respected around town, and I have no reason to believe that he and Ellie aren't lovebirds."

"Your background knowledge of Mr. Roeder is impressive."

"I poked around a bit after I did a story about him calling an executive session of the Erin Airport Board. Under Ohio law, any public body can hold an executive session only after voting to do that, by roll call vote, and the vote has to be a public meeting. Hardly anybody attends the public meetings of small boards anyway, which is why I sometimes do when I'm at City Hall or the county building and I see that one is going on. I figure that somebody should be watching. Well, I happened to be there when the airport board voted to go into executive session."

"Why did they go into executive session?" I had to ask.

"You tell me and we'll both know, Jeff. The motion said something like 'in accordance with Section Thus and So of the Ohio Revised Code.' I looked up the section at the time and the wording there could cover anything from disciplining a public official to buying or selling property. So, I guess it was legal, but that didn't make it right. The public's business should be done in public, not in secret. So, I wrote a story about it."

"And the reaction was?" Mac asked.

"Probably the only reader who didn't yawn was Vance Roeder. He got on his high horse and told me my story was bad for Erin. He should be a politician."

We were going down a rabbit hole here, and I burrowed still deeper despite the glazed look on Oscar's face. "It seems like much ado about nothing. I mean, this is the Erin Municipal Airport we're talking about."

Our little airport, about 300 acres surrounded by fallow farmland, services mostly corporate aircraft—notably that of the ever-growing Altiora Corp.—but also occasionally private and charter planes from our southwest corner of Ohio. Nearby Lunken Airport (officially Cincinnati Municipal Airport–Lunken Field) was a landing spot for Charles Lindbergh and the Beatles in different eras, but I don't think Erin Municipal ever saw the likes of them.

"It's the principle that counts, Jeff," Johanna assured me. "And it's local news. Do you realize that local news reporting is dying in this country?"

"Well, yes, Lynda—"

"Newspapers are closing every week." *Small colleges too!* "And dozens of papers in small towns like ours actually don't have a single reporter!"

"How is that even possible?" Mac asked.

"Outsourcing. They rely entirely on freelancers and stories from the parent company, outfits like Gannett and Grier. Our staff is tiny, but at least we have one. Without reporters on the beat, who will catch the corruption? Thank the journalism gods for Serena Mason buying the *Observer*!"

Chapter Twenty
Next to Die?

"SERENA MASON," MAC MULLED. "She moves in much the same circles as Arthur Vance Roeder. Perhaps she would have some insight about that gentleman." This was back in his Chevy after we civilians had all left Oscar's office—Johanna first, followed shortly by Mac and me.

"So, since Roeder has no known connection to Quant, are you focusing on what you called Scenario Two, the idea that the two murders were unrelated? And are you thinking that maybe Roeder had what you would call an amorous relationship with Dixie Parks that could be hazardous to his wealth, given that his wife has all the money? Is that what you're doing?"

"What I am doing is grasping at straws, Jefferson!"

"Well, you don't have to get snippy about it."

THE MASON RESIDENCE IS a 160-year-old Victorian number. Built by one of Serena's late husband's ancestors, the railroad baron who founded that family fortune, it has a gazebo in the back and substantial acreage. Serena also "came from money," as they say, although these days she spends a lot of her time giving it away through the Mason Foundation.

We found her in her garden with a shovel in her hand and a determined look on her face, a short woman with hair more salt than pepper. Never mind that she could afford a whole platoon of gardeners and her age is somewhere north of 80. Apparently, she's one of those people who comes alive when digging in dirt. My mother was like that before she was confined to a wheelchair, although she is a poet of no small reputation.

After pleasantries, Mac introduced the subject of our visit:

"A woman named Dixie Parks was shot to death in her own home last night," he said.

"I know. I was in the *Observer* newsroom earlier today. What an awful thing! But you're here for a reason, not to play town crier." Nobody ever called Serena Mason slow on the uptake.

"Mrs. Parks was executive assistant to Arthur Vance Roeder. We thought that you might know him."

"I've known Vance my whole life," Serena said, wiping perspiration off her face. She's too rich to sweat. "In fact, we're third cousins. We both married up."

"Financially or otherwise?" Mac asked.

Serena's birth family was a branch of the old Kozinn department store dynasty out of Cincinnati, well-heeled but not in the Mason class.

"I meant we both have—or had, in my case—wonderful spouses."

"Sad, is it not, that some individuals do not appreciate the blessings of their life?"

He didn't have to draw Serena a map.

"I'm certain that Vance is very devoted to Ellie," she said. "If he weren't, I would have heard about it. That sort of news travels fast in my crowd."

This did not shock me.

"He seems to have been quite close to the late Mrs. Parks," Mac said.

"I'm close to a lot of people, male and female. Look, I've played poker with Vance enough to know that if he were stepping out on Ellie, she could read it on his face like a newspaper headline."

An appropriate metaphor for the owner and publisher of the *Observer*, I thought!

Since we were talking about the local bluebloods, I asked, "Do you know Carson Kincade? We kind of ran into him on the golf course yesterday."

Mac winced at the memory of that debacle.

"Our paths have crossed," Serena said in a way that somehow made me feel like that was an understatement. "I've always felt that Carson was a man running to catch up with his father, Andrew, who was a very successful investor related to the Harridans on his mother's side. He's harmless if you don't give him anything important to do.

"So, Mac, we've got two unsolved murders in our little town. Sometimes I wonder how our per capital homicide rate compares to New York or Chicago." *You really don't want to know, Serena.* "I don't suppose the latest killings are related?"

"That remains an open question," Mac informed her. "Mrs. Parks was a client of the woman who called herself Mistress Quant. It could be a coincidence that two women who knew each other were murdered in close proximity. Or it could be that the two were killed for the same motive. Or it could be . . ." He stopped, apparently surprised by his own thoughts, then finished the sentence: "It could be that Mrs.

Parks's death is related to her being a Witch's Brew patron, in which case other clients could be in danger."

"Well, be sure to let Johanna know when you—I mean, when Chief Hummel identifies the killer or killers. I want the *Observer* to have the story before the Associated Press or PNN."

"SO, IF DIXIE PARKS wasn't killed by her husband, and if her murder is related to the Quant murder, it could be because she saw or heard or figured out something that puts the killer in danger. And if she was able to do that because she was a Quant client, then the other clients could be in danger."

"Well summarized, Jefferson!"

"But we have no way of knowing who entered that shop! The place has to be full of fingerprints, and not all of them would be on record somewhere."

"Very true. We do, however, know of two other tarot clients. I feel a responsibility to warn them of their possible danger. One or both of them could be the next to die."

This conversation took place in the Macmobile, which took up a considerable amount of space in the long Mason driveway in which we were parked. Mac took out his cell and called Brie Weatherby.

"You again!" was her response to his "Sebastian McCabe calling."

"Please do not hang up!"

He gave her the spiel.

"Look, McCabe, do you think I haven't racked my brains trying to think of anything I might know that could help the cops find Mistress Quant's killer? It's kept me awake at night."

"Perhaps you know something that you do not know you know."

"And perhaps you are a—"

"It is also possible that the killer thinks you know something you do not," Mac interrupted. "Be careful, Ms. Weatherby. Be very careful."

Without responding to that, Weatherby hung up.

"That went well," I said.

Knowing that Jade Lazelle was on the job at Bobbie McGee's and not likely available by phone even if we had her number, we managed to grab a few minutes with her there without ordering a meal this time.

"But that's crazy!" she told us after Mac had quickly filled her in on the possibility that she could be number three on the murderer's hit parade. "I have no idea who killed Mistress Quant."

"Have you thought about it?" Mac asked.

"Well, not really. But like I told you, I only had that one session with her."

"Perhaps you should think about it and tell me or the police if you come up with anything. It may be something you saw, or something Ms. Quant said." He gave her his business card. "And be careful. Be very careful."

Chapter Twenty-One
The Office Spouse

HERBERT HALL, WHERE MAC'S office is located, is between the parking lot and my office, so we walked that far together. We were some yards away from the classic Federal-style building when I saw the familiar figure of PNN icon Bennington Lee standing in front. Set up next to him was a camera on a tripod, manned—or rather womanned—by a middle-aged cameraperson wearing one of those down jackets with no sleeves and lots of pockets.

"If we go around the back—" I began.

"Nonsense, old boy!"

Having met us previously in that St. Patrick's Day mess some years back, Lee presented himself as an old friend and promised that he only wanted a few words with Mac. That meant about 15 minutes, several of which might actually be used because *American Scene*'s niche is relatively in-depth reports by TV standards.

Some highlights that made the final cut that evening on PNN:

"Professor McCabe, would it be fair to say that you are involved in this double mystery?"

"It would certainly not be unfair. It would be accurate to the extent that I knew both of the victims."

"But you are also involved in trying to find the killer—isn't that true?"

"I have every confidence that Chief Hummel and his excellent officers will identify the killer and bring him or her to justice."

At this point Lee looked a little frustrated by the verbal jousting.

"With your help, don't you mean?" he prodded.

"Every citizen has a duty to help the police."

To his credit, Lee tried another ploy.

"Do you think the two murders are related?"

"At this time, that is unclear. However, it is safe to say that if the two murders are related, and we learn how they are related, then we will most probably know the identity of the killer."

"So that's your focus?" Lee asked, but it sounded more like an exclamation in an "*Aha!*" tone of voice. "How the two murders are related, if they are related?"

"Our focus is finding the killer, Mr. Lee. Or rather, that is law enforcement's focus."

"WHAT A LOT OF hot air!" was Lynda's reaction when we watched *American Scene* that night.

"Not all of it, Lyn," I corrected. "Only the part about Mac expecting Oscar to find the killer. All the rest is true."

"I wish I'd interviewed Dixie Parks for my upcoming someday 'Witch Is Dead' podcast," she ruminated. "That might have yielded a clue. So where is Mac casting his line next?"

"Back to Arthur Vance Roeder."

Lynda bit her lip in thought. "I thought you said Serena threw cold water on him as a suspect."

"She did. But Mac's latest shot in the dark is that he may know who Dixie's new boyfriend was. Said boyfriend might have had a fatal argument with her or, if not, at least have important information that's germane to the murder even though he's reluctant to come forward and get caught in the crossfire."

Cincinnati's TV4 news with Brian Rose and Tammie Tucker gave the Parks murder as much attention as they had Quant's demise. So did Channel 11 (*Live@11 on TV11!*), with reporter Jason Sanchez solemnly intoning to their anchor, "Yes, Jessica, murder has once again come to the quiet river town of Erin, Ohio. And the victim was associated with a woman killed just last week"—dramatic pause—"a woman who identified as a witch."

The print media were generally more restrained, but not always. Lynda and I checked out the online versions before lights-out for the night. It wasn't ideal bedtime reading.

WITCH'S CLIENT MURDERED was the headline somebody chose for Johanna's story online, which began: "A woman known to be a client of the late Zoraida Quant, murdered last week, was herself shot in the head . . ." Joe Ziebart and Deidre Chandler, in the *Cincinnati Sentinel*, went with a more sensational take, true to form for the online-only news outlet: "A tarot card reading by the late Zoraida Quant apparently didn't warn Dixie Parks . . ." Morris Kindle of the Associated Press stuck to the more old-fashioned just-the-facts approach: "The body of 45-year-old Dixie Parks, shot through the head, was found . . ."

"How does the *Sentinel* know that a tarot reading didn't warn Parks?" Lynda kvetched. "It could have warned her to no effect. The *Observer* had much better coverage anyway. Johanna reported that the coroner said the gun was a .38 and that the death is consistent with the time gunshots were heard Sunday night, plus Oscar's comment about canvassing the neighborhood to see if anybody saw anything around that time. Isn't it exciting that she's engaged, darling?"

POPCORN, HAVING CONSUMED all of the aforementioned media, and no doubt at least a partial debriefing from Oscar, was still breathless for all the details I hadn't had a chance to share with her yesterday. She wanted it all.

"He's not that good an Elvis," was her comment on Luke Parks.

"You saw him at a bachelorette party?"

"Retirement. Hilda Crowens in the History Department."

"Isn't she old enough to have been the real Elvis's babysitter?"

"Almost."

And so forth.

But we managed to get some work done before Mac and I took off at lunchtime for a talk with Vance Roeder.

THIS WAS OUR SECOND trip to the Winfield Hotel in less than a week, but that was no burden to an architecture buff like me. It's an art deco masterpiece that wouldn't be out of place in a much larger city, built at a time when an earlier generation of Winfields expected Erin to grow and wanted to get ahead of the curve. Which was also an era when hotels were beautiful, not just functional. Have I ever told you that I love art deco?

We had gotten no further than the lobby, ornately decorated with images of civic progress in Rookwood tile, when we saw Ralph Pendergast and Carson Kincade coming our way. Was that an "oh, no!" expression on Ralph's face? Kincade, dressed in a sport coat, tie, chinos, and expensive loafers, was friendlier but didn't mean it.

"Hello, gentlemen," was his opening line, delivered with a phony smile. Then he quickly shifted moods, becoming solemn. "We were just here to tell Vance how sorry we were to hear about Dix's death. Murder!" He shook his head. "Hard to believe. I mean, we saw her every time we visited Vance! I presume you've inserted yourself into this police investigation as well, McCabe. I hope you do better than last time."

This reference to Mac's embarrassing misfire on the links two days before, delivered with what I would call a nasty tone and all the subtlety of a pile driver, would have flattened a lesser man. But my brother-in-law remained unmoved.

"I am sure Mr. Roeder appreciates your condolences," he said. "We are here to visit him as well."

"We met your niece, Madam Lena," I informed Ralph.

He winced. "I had hopes that she would make more of her life than living on a houseboat and reading palms."

"Her student loans are paid off," I told him, in case he didn't know. "She'll do fine."

"MR. PARKS TELLS US that his wife had a new love in her life," Mac said. "Do you know whether that is true?"

"I suspected it," Roeder said with a sigh. "She was dressing better and seemed happier."

"And yet," Mac said, "if you only suspected, that means she did not give you a name. Was Mrs. Parks reticent about her private life?"

"Not especially. Not to me, after working closely together for sixteen years. We didn't see each other much outside of the office, but we were together a good part of every day, sometimes into the evening, and we talked a lot. She told me more about visiting that fortune teller than I wanted to know." He shook his head. "I still can't believe somebody killed her. How's the police investigation going?"

"I assure you that Chief Hummel will not rest until Mrs. Parks's killer is found. Jefferson and I will do our best to help in an unofficial capacity."

"Hence your visit and your question." Roeder sighed again. "There must have been some reason she didn't tell me about this boyfriend, now that I think about it." He seemed kind of stuck on that, maybe feeling out of the loop.

"Clearly, it was not you."

"Clearly," Roeder snapped, either offended or giving a good imitation of it. "I'm very happily married."

To the owner of the hotel that employs me.

"I am sure you must be tortured by the fact that had you been working in the office with Mrs. Parks last night she might be alive now."

Although that might be true, Mac was really asking where Roeder was at the time of the murder without asking where Roeder was at the time of the murder. And Roeder gave it to him:

"It has occurred to me, yes. For a good part of the evening, between seven and nine, I was on a Zoom call—a meeting of an ad hoc committee to get public art downtown." Mac raised an eyebrow. Kate was gung-ho on that idea, as I knew from hearing her hold forth on it more than once. I made a mental note to suggest to Roeder that she be added to the committee, since Mac's eyebrow action suggested that he didn't know about it.

"Who else was on the call?"

"The mayor, Jacqui Daniel, Carson Kincade, Arlo Bainbridge, Adam Mendenhall from the art museum, and Dante Peter O'Neill."

That last-named individual is the dean of SBU's School of Arts and Humanities. Altogether, a more rock-solid list of citizens would be hard to find in Erin. And they were Arthur Vance Roeder's alibi for Dixie Parks's murder.

Chapter Twenty-Two
Connections and Secrets

"A REAL P.I. WOULD wear out shoe leather proving that Roeder and Parks"—that sounded like a law firm—"were a hot item during secret trips to Cincinnati and Licking Falls or someplace really romantic, like Barbados," I told Mac on the way back to his vehicle.

I should know, having written multiple (unpublished) private eye novels.

"Do you really believe such unsavory trysts were going on, Jefferson?"

Mac fired up a cigar as we walked, making me glad we were in the open air.

"Not really," I admitted. "Aside from appearing to be a decent sort, Roeder is married to his job, you might say. And if I read him correctly, he wouldn't risk that. Also, he has an alibi for the time of Dixie Parks's murder, as do all the other people on that Zoom call. Wait a minute! We should check that out. Roeder could have made it up on the spot. Of all the people he said were on the call, who's the most reliable and also not a blabbermouth?"

The question practically answered itself! As we climbed into his Chevy, Mac called Reverend Mayor Fred Sutterlee, who confirmed the meeting and Arthur Vance

Roeder's active participation in it, along with all those other local big names.

"I believe we have made some real progress in developing a plan to create public art downtown to enrich and enliven our community," that worthy enthused.

Good to know. Meanwhile, back to the murder investigation.

Suddenly, I had a brainstorm to ask our clerical mayor, "Do you know Reverend Adam Sapp?"

Sapp's name hadn't come up in connection with the death of Dixie Parks. Therefore, if this were one of Mac's Damon Devlin mystery novels, he would almost surely be the killer.

"That I do! He is an active member of our ministerial association."

"What do you think of him?"

"A righteous man with an unfortunate taste in music."

Before I could ask whether "righteous" translated into "would stone a witch" or "wouldn't stone a witch," Mayor Sutterlee asked about the state of the investigation into the two murders.

"It would be accurate to say that it is quite active," Mac assured him.

That drew a chuckle. "Well, then, I will continue to hold your efforts and those of the police in prayer."

"WHERE DOES THAT LEAVE US?" I asked Mac after he expressed his thanks for the prayer (not saying how much we needed it) and disconnected.

"Approximately nowhere. Not only does Mr. Roeder have an alibi for the time of Mrs. Parks's death, but we also have no real reason to believe that they were romantically involved. I am afraid that we must reconsider that old cliché of the Woman Who Knew Too Much—the possibility that Mrs. Parks was killed because she knew who killed Zoraida Quant."

"Then why did it take almost a week for the killer to eliminate the threat?"

"An excellent question, indeed!" Mac blew cigar smoke meditatively. "Perhaps the killer was Mrs. Parks's new love, and he was confident that she was so smitten with him she would keep his secret—but for some reason decided he could not suffer that risk."

"Zane Quant!" I blurted out.

"Bravo, Jefferson! A creditable suggestion. The victim's offspring profits by his estranged mother's death, and in theory he could have been Mrs. Parks's unknown lover. Unfortunately, you will recall that Colonel Gibbons said his alibi checked out, along with that of Reverend Sapp. Mr. Quant was at a school open house, and then with a number of friends for drinks, where his lack of generosity in sharing the tab was apparently notable."

"Oh."

"I suggest we call it an afternoon and reconvene this evening in my study."

"Come over to my place. I'm watching the kids tonight while Lynda's out."

IN REALITY, DONATA, SAM, and Jake watch each other until a referee is needed. Lynda and I are strong believers in child's play, and not all on computers. On this particular evening, Donata's buddy and next-door neighbor Andy Patch was also part of the circus.

So, after a late afternoon highlighted by a call from Hadley Reams of *Observer* for a story about sorority consultants who advise young women on style and social skills during rush—and hey, if there are empty-nester coaches, why not sorority consultants?—I had dinner with Lynda and the kids, sent Lynda off with hugs and kisses, and shortly thereafter welcomed Mac.

"May we use your computer?" he asked.

"I thought that would be on the agenda. Come into my office."

I already had the laptop set up. Ever since the COVID shutdown of four years earlier I've referred to our screened-in porch as my home office. Because it is. Lynda has a long-established office of her own, with a real desk, in our fourth bedroom.

"This is the part of the case where we make a chart, right?" I asked.

"I prefer to call it a table," Mac said.

"With suspects, alibis, motives, stuff like that?"

"I propose that we take a new approach."

"Eh? What else is there?"

"Connections, old boy! Relationships! The key question here is what ties the two murders together. It occurs to me that in some way or other, the link must be a person. In the trifling matter of Seth Miller's stolen bicycle and the consequent pawn shop robbery, the perpetrator became obvious by his connection to both victims. He worked out at Nouveau Shape with Seth, and he was a customer of Long John Gold. This will be a much more subtle matter. What I propose is to show connections among our various dramatis personae in tabular form. One degree of separation should be sufficient."

"Give me a for-instance."

"Very well. The odious Luke Parks is one degree of separation from both Carson Kincade and Arthur Vance Roeder because he knew Dixie Parks—in the Biblical sense, in that case—and she knew each of those other gentlemen to different degrees. Further removed connections would be unhelpful as well as problematical. For example, Jade Lazelle, as a restaurant server, must know hundreds of individuals at a surface level, and each of them know many more. All sorts of social connections are possible but unhelpful.

"On this chart, I will rule out Ms. Quant's Instagram targets as being too remote a link unless there is also a connection to someone else on the chart. And I will mark an 'X' if there is no known connection. Bear in mind, however, that we are talking one degree of separation, meaning that two individuals know a third person in common. Although they may not know each other, that possibility exists—and it may have been a fatal knowledge. Also, I will take the liberty of listing Mr. Kincade's connection to Ms. Quant through Instagram, although that is not a person. Mr. Roeder was also connected to her in the same way, but more concretely through Dixie Parks."

Got all that?

Mac's fingers flew over the laptop until they produced:

Quant/Parks Connections

	Carson Kincade	Jade Lazelle	Dixie Parks	Luke Parks	Zoraida Quant	Arthur Vance Roeder	Brie Weatherby
Carson Kincade		X	Arthur Vance Roeder	Dixie Parks	Dixie Parks	Civic activities	X
Jade Lazelle	X		Zoraida Quant	Dixie Parks	Client	Dixie Parks	Zoraida Quant
Dixie Parks	Arthur Vance Roeder	Zoraida Quant		Spouse	Client	Boss	Zoraida Quant
Luke Parks	Dixie Parks	Dixie Parks	Spouse		Dixie Parks	Dixie Parks	Dixie Parks
Zoraida Quant	Dixie Parks	Client	Client	Dixie Parks		Dixie Parks	Client
Arthur Vance Roeder	Civic activities	Dixie Parks	Exec Assistant	Dixie Parks	Dixie Parks		Dixie Parks
Brie Weatherby	X	Zoraida Quant	Zoraida Quant	Dixie Parks	Client	Dixie Parks	

"This chart is telling us something, Jefferson!"

It's telling me I have a headache.

After some thought, I said:

"It shows that Dixie Parks had connections either directly or through another person to—in order across the top of the chart—Kincade, Lazelle, her husband, Quant of course, Roeder, and Weatherby. That's everybody on the chart. Likewise, Quant had connections to Lazelle, Weatherby, Dixie and through Dixie to Luke Parks, Kincade and Roeder. Okay. But what about Robin Hauser, the Quant siblings, and Adam Sapp?"

"All of those had theoretical reasons, however unlikely, to kill Ms. Quant without one degree of separation to someone else in the case. Hence, no need to put them on the table."

Mac studied said table.

"Ms. Quant was Dixie Parks's confidant," he added after a while. "Her exact words to us were, 'I could tell her anything. And I did.'"

"That might mean something if Quant were the second victim—she might have known something that would lead to the killer of Parks, making her your mythical Woman Who Knew Too Much. But Quant died first!"

When Sebastian McCabe has a train of thought, it is not easily derailed.

"Nevertheless, Jefferson, as a thought experiment, what if Ms. Quant were killed for knowing something?"

"Quant had already told you and the prosecutor something she knew—that Troy Braggs killed Betty Erlanger," I objected. "Maybe Oscar's right and it was as simple as that: Quant was killed to stop her from testifying and Parks was killed for a completely unrelated reason, or because she knew something that could point to Quant's killer. Robin Hauser has no real alibi except her cat."

"And not a scintilla of evidence against her," Mac volleyed back. "You make a good point, however. Ms. Quant had already come to me and was willing to testify in court against Troy Braggs. In fact, she made a sworn statement. What else could she know? And why not tell it? Perhaps she did not know what she knew. Or perhaps—"

He stopped, with a look on his bearded face that I've seen there many times before, a sort of "now I get it!" expression.

"—perhaps what she knew pertained to something that had not yet happened! Suppose the killer realized that

Zoraida Quant would know or strongly suspect the motive behind Mrs. Parks's death, and therefore the killer, after the murder happened. So, he killed Ms. Quant first."

Mac was flying along now, and I was barely holding on.

"How would Quant know this motive?" I asked.

"Because Mrs. Parks told her intimate things during their tarot card sessions, quite likely including the identity of her new love interest."

"Which was a secret to everybody else, as far as we can tell."

"Yes, a secret!" Mac all but shouted. "Everyone has secrets, do they not? When did we hear that word recently?"

"Yesterday. Johanna said it."

"Right you are, Jefferson! Now I recall. Admirable journalist that she is, she said, 'The public's business should be done in public, not in secret.' She was referring to the airport board's executive session. Who heads the airport board? Arthur Vance Roeder. Who is likely to know what that secret session was all about? His invaluable executive assistant, Mrs. Parks. And she must have shared that knowledge with her new love interest, who then . . . Of course! My instinct was correct, old boy. The answer is concealed here on our table within one degree of separation."

Mac used the "draw" function in Word to highlight how two people were connected by a third.

"That conjunction of names has stimulated a memory for me," Mac said. "I now distinctly recall that this one"— Mac pointed with the cursor to a name—"referred to Mrs. Parks by what could only be an affectionate nickname that we heard no one else use for her. Those two were what used to be called, and perhaps still is, an 'item'."

I've been around too long to be shocked, but I still didn't get it.

"So, how did that lead to murder?" I had to ask.

He told me.

"But the alibi!" I protested.

"I think we can eliminate that obstacle with a call to the mayor."

After getting the answer he wanted, and expected, from Reverend Sutterlee, Mac made one more call—to Grant Kingsley, SBU president and former Altiora Corp. executive.

Chapter Twenty-Three
The Woman Who Knew Too Much

"WHAT ARE WE DOING at this dinky airport?" Carson Kincade demanded.

"It is indeed small," Mac acknowledged. "However, the killer knows it is soon to get larger, a change that is highly significant to this case. It is, in fact, the motive."

"You're shitting me!" That was Arthur Vance Roeder, not looking at all happy to be there that Wednesday morning along with Jade Lazelle, Brie Weatherby, Zoe and Zane Quant, Tall Rawls, and, of course, the local forces of law and order. If any of them wondered why Mac had a laptop in his hand, they didn't say so. We were standing in the beautiful 1930s-era airport terminal, yet another art deco building and well preserved.

"Why are we here?" Zane Quant, the science teacher, demanded. His sister, the death doula, looked equally curious but willing to go with the flow.

"Didn't you learn anything from that cockup on the golf course Sunday?" Roeder added, pointedly addressing this to Mac.

Oscar looked puzzled, not being privy to that disaster. Mac ignored Roeder and steamed on:

"In my early speculation about the possible scenarios for Mrs. Parks's death, I included 'none of the above.' And, indeed, that was the case. The two murders were not unrelated, they did not have the same motive, and Mrs. Parks was not The Woman Who Knew Too Much. However, Zoraida Quant *did* threaten the killer with her knowledge—or would have if she were not silenced."

"I thought sure one of those doofuses she went after on Instagram killed her," Lazelle said.

"And you were correct. However, Ms. Quant's video assaults on the man had nothing to do with it.

"Carson Kincade killed her. He killed her because he assumed, no doubt correctly, that her client, Dixie Parks, would have shared with her in confidence the fact that she was romantically involved with him—a relationship that would automatically make Mr. Kincade a strong suspect in the murder of Mrs. Parks that he was already planning."

"What! You asshole." Kincade wasn't exactly flapping, but he was no longer unflappable. The controlled manner that fit so well with his put-together look had taken a hike.

"If there was a clue in the tarot cards, which seems rather beside the point now, it was in the card called 'The Lovers,'[14] Mac said.

"What do you mean, clue?" Johanna demanded.

"Yeah, what?" Weatherby echoed.

"We'll catch you up later," I told Johanna.

Meanwhile, Roeder's expression had gone from stunned to regarding Kincade the way I regard a bad day for my retirement portfolio.

"Is that true, Carson?" he demanded.

---

[14] As both Mac (p. 121) and I (p. 129) had speculated earlier.

"No. Of course not! It's nonsense. Again. Just like Sunday." Speaking in a measured voice, Kincade had recovered his aplomb. "What makes you think Dixie Parks and I were more than nodding acquaintances who crossed paths occasionally at Vance's office?"

"When we encountered you in the lobby of the Winfield, you said you had come to express your sympathy to Mr. Roeder about 'Dix's death.' No one else that we know of called Mrs. Parks 'Dix'—not her estranged husband nor her employer with whom she spent most of her working hours for sixteen years as his executive assistant."

"I never heard her called that," Roeder confirmed in an ice-cold tone.

"It was clearly what is colloquially called a 'pet name,' showing a familiarity that could be simply friendship. However, your denial of anything more than a passing acquaintance with Mrs. Parks just ruled out that innocent interpretation. Thank you."

Nice touch, that last!

As Kincade looked at the faces around him, including Oscar and Gibbons, the term "cornered rat" occurred to me. But he was a calculating rodent.

"Well, what if we were more than casual acquaintances?" he demanded. "As a practical matter, we were both available but didn't want to make our relationship public until her divorce was final. That hardly means I had reason to kill her. Just the opposite!"

"Available?" Mac repeated. His ability to load a single word with sarcasm impressed even me, and sarcasm is my superpower. "The more accurate word for Mrs. Parks at that point was 'vulnerable,' and you took advantage of that to exploit her. The key to the true nature of your relationship, from your perverse perspective, is that you knew each other through Mr. Roeder, a connection which became clear to me when Jefferson and I made this table."

He opened up the laptop and showed them.

Quant/Parks Connections

	Carson Kincade	Jade Lazelle	Dixie Parks	Luke Parks	Zoraida Quant	Arthur Vance Roeder	Brie Weatherby
Carson Kincade		X	Arthur Vance Roeder	Dixie Parks	Dixie Parks	Civic activities	X
Jade Lazelle	X		Zoraida Quant	Dixie Parks	Client	X	Zoraida Quant
Dixie Parks	Arthur Vance Roeder	Zoraida Quant		Spouse	Client	Boss	Zoraida Quant
Luke Parks	Dixie Parks	Dixie Parks	Spouse		Dixie Parks	Dixie Parks	Dixie Parks
Zoraida Quant	Dixie Parks	Client	Client	Dixie Parks		Dixie Parks	Client
Arthur Vance Roeder	Civic activities	Dixie Parks	Exec Assistant	Dixie Parks	Dixie Parks		Dixie Parks
Brie Weatherby	X	Zoraida Quant	Zoraida Quant	Dixie Parks	Client	Dixie Parks	

"As you can see, I have drawn a link—quite literally—from Mrs. Parks to Mr. Kincade through Mr. Roeder. The Roeder connection was the key. The pair met during Mr. Kincade's visits to Mr. Roeder's office at the Winfield. If that was the extent of their relationship, that would have meant nothing. But an intimate alliance meant that the executive secretary might share her employer's confidences in an unguarded moment, which is why Mr. Kincade cultivated her.

Mrs. Parks' comprehensive knowledge of Mr. Roeder's affairs, professional and volunteer, made her the perfect insider source."

"Source of what? Where is all this going?" The question came from Weatherby. Maybe she was worried about her own "shared confidences" during "intimate alliances."

"Mr. Kincade was fairly described by the late Ms. Quant in one of her videos as a 'dabbler who spends more than he has.' Using inherited wealth, he has invested in real estate with only modest success while apparently living at a high level that includes frequent cruises, according to his assistant. Perhaps he is better at golf than at business. One of his golfing friends is Mr. Roeder, which is why Mr. Kincade occasionally visited him at his office, perhaps to meet before going out to lunch."

"Are you implying—" Roeder began.

"Nothing nefarious or injudicious on your part," Mac assured him. "I suspect that at some point, on the links or over a friendly meal, you made some allusion to the executive session of the Erin Airport Board without saying what it was about. Mr. Kincade sensed a business opportunity if he could come to know what others did not, which is why he needed to get closer to Mrs. Parks. As Jefferson pointed out to me, executive assistants know everything. She specifically mentioned to us your work on the airport board. And Mr. Kincade was probably aware from you, Mr. Roeder, that she was going through a divorce and therefore particularly susceptible to his attentions."

"It's a big expansion," Roeder blurted out. "That's what the executive session was about. More than one, actually. The airport board is going to buy up a lot of that farm-land around it and make the airport bigger to handle the increased air traffic generated by Altiora. The reason we went into executive session to talk about it is that the price of land will skyrocket once word gets out that we have our wallet open. Classic supply and demand. We tried to keep it hush-hush to save the taxpayers' money."

Mac had suspected the airport expansion, and GK confirmed on the phone that he'd heard strong rumors along those lines from contacts at Altiora, his former employer.

"And Mr. Kincade, not unintelligent despite being unsuccessful, quickly realized that he could buy land at today's prices from the unsuspecting owners and force the airport board to pay him a premium to acquire it from him. That would allow him to restore his depleted fortune and live up to the image of success he has long cultivated."

"But why kill Dixie?" Roeder asked.

"Because if his advance notice of the airport expansion became known—which could happen if Mrs. Parks ever became disaffected with him—that would unwind his profits. Section 121.22(6) of the Ohio Revised Code provides that the sale of the property he intended to buy could be undone by the knowledge that he had covert information of the airport expansion before he bought it. I confirmed this by accessing the Ohio Revised Code on the Ohio.gov website. Mr. Kincade must have known that law from being involved in real estate projects, albeit at a modest level."

Kincade finally thought of something to say:

"That fantasy sounds like something out of one of your books." *Actually, Carson, it's from one of my books—the one you're in.* "You know I have an alibi when Dixie was murdered. I was on a Zoom call with Vance and other distinguished citizens, including the mayor, in a meeting of an ad hoc committee on public art."

Mac nodded. "That was certainly the perception. However, on a Zoom call one is not talking all the time, and one is not required to show one's face. Earlier in this case I reflected to Chief Hummel and Jefferson that even though a certain suspect could prove she was streaming television programs while Ms. Quant was being killed, she had no way to verify that she was actually watching those programs. The situation with Zoom is somewhat analogous: Being signed in does not prove that one is actually there. So, I called Mayor Sutterlee last night, established that the meeting of the public art committee was recorded, and looked at the recording. You were on a cell phone during that meeting, Mr. Kincade, and there was a half-hour period during which a photograph of you replaced your live visage and you did not speak."

"That proves nothing!"

"Nor does the fact that I am sure surveillance tapes from the Forty Thieves Casino will not support your story that you were gambling there the night of Ms. Quant's murder. Your lack of alibi for either murder does, however, create the possibility of your guilt.

"More telling is the fact that county records"—*thank you, Ms. Ziv!*—"show that you have begun to buy property surrounding the airport, which you funded by selling a number of rental properties, including the building in which the Witch's Brew was located. I would not be surprised to find out that your home is also newly mortgaged.

"All of that is merely indicative. As for real proof, I strongly suspect that, lacking contacts to buy an illegal gun, you purchased one legally, of which there will be a record."

"There is," Gibbons chimed in, speaking for the first time. "Mr. Kincade bought a .38 three weeks ago. We'll need to compare it with the bullets removed from the body. We have a search warrant for the Kincade home."

"I might have misplaced the gun," Kincade said. *Translation: You'd have to drag the Ohio River to find it.* "I was going to take up target shooting but I lost interest."

"The instrument of death in Ms. Quant's murder was a rock or stone, which seemed to match the biblical injunction about stoning witches. You would know about that from the Reverend Sapp's Instagram video, to which you referred. I believe your words to me were, 'That Adam Sapp guy took on Quant in his own video.' Are there rocks in your garden, Mr. Kincade?"

"I'm not saying anything more until I get a lawyer."

But he didn't need to. He had answered the question by not answering it.

"I'm pretty sure there are rocks in your garden, or somewhere in your yard—fossilized sedimentary rocks matching the one that killed Zoraida Quant," Oscar said, "Carson Kincade, you are under arrest. You have the right to remain silent . . ."

Chapter Twenty-Four
Character Clues

"THE SIGN SAYS 'MISTRESS QUANT'S Witches Brew,' and below that the description 'metaphysical supply shop.' We are standing outside the deserted building now. A peek through the cobwebbed windows gives a view of crystals, charms, tarot cards, and pagan ritual items. It was here on a September morning in 2024 that Brie Weatherby saw the bloodied body of a murder victim—a woman well known as a witch."

So began Lynda's "The Witch Is Dead" podcast, written and produced by her as a freelancer and distributed through her former employer, Grier Media Group, so that she doesn't have to handle the nitty gritty of that part. Oscar, Jade Lazelle, Brie Weatherby, Madam Lena, Luke Parks, and Kincade's former personal assistant Lulu Thatcher had been happy to cooperate; Carson Kincade, Arthur Vance Roeder, and all three surviving Quants, not so much.

Lynda wasn't happy about not being invited to the soiree where Mac unveiled the murderer; she would have loved to record the whole thing for her podcast. But to make up for it, Mac agreed to answer any questions (as if she could stop him!) and re-enact anything she asked.

The sale of the Witch's Brew building to Gulliver Mackie had gone through as planned (although Kincade now needed the money for his defense, not for buying land to re-sell to the airport board), and Mackie gave Lynda the key to the building before the new tenant took over. So, for atmospherics, that's where she had her final interview with Mac—the scene of the first murder. That's where he'd noticed the tarot cards that may or may not have been intended as a clue to the murderer (personally, I think not) but certainly had no role in solving the crime.

First, Lynda recorded those opening minutes outside, then they entered the shuttered shop to talk. I went along for the ride. They'd earlier gone to the Erin Municipal Airport to record there. Apparently, the atmospherics count in a podcast even though listeners can't see the various locations.

"Ironically, it was all about Carson Kincade and real estate, after all—just not in the way I had originally speculated that day at the golf course," he said near the end of the session at the shop. Lynda had convinced him to come clean about that fiasco, arguing (with a straight face) that it would add to the suspense and make his ultimate triumph even more spectacular. "There was much more at stake than getting an inconvenient tenant out of the way in order to smooth the way for a sale of the building."

By this time, Oscar's forces had established that the rocks in the garden behind Kincade's house—where, by the way, he had entertained Dixie so that her neighbors would never see him—did match the one that killed Zoraida Quant.

"The brutal method of murder normally would indicate great passion," Mac told Lynda and her future podcast listeners. "In this case, however, it was a calculated red herring designed to throw suspicion on Reverend Sapp because of his reference to stoning witches on his Instagram channel.

Mr. Kincade knew about that and referred to it in conversation with me. Naturally, he chose an entirely different method of murdering his unfortunate paramour, in hopes of concealing the connection between the two crimes. However, the attempt to make the killing of Dixie Parks look like a burglary was botched, as were so many of Mr. Kincade's projects. Chief Hummel, although preferring the 'robbery gone wrong' scenario instinctively, was not fooled."

"As my close friend and brother-in-law Thomas Jefferson Cody observed during the course of our investigation, personal assistants know everything about their bosses. That applied to both Dixie Parks and to Lulu Thatcher. And Ms. Thatcher told us that Carson Kincade did not do much. That was all too true—he is a bungler who has managed to piffle away a medium-sized fortune, as Ms. Quant observed on one of her Instagram videos. In fact, I suspect he was motivated in this tragic course more by the need to redeem himself than to make money. I suppose you might say there were many character clues pointing to the killer."

"Were there other clues you haven't mentioned yet?"

After a moment's thought, Mac came up with one that I suppose you could say was another character clue of sorts.

"To be candid, I did not realize until later the significance of Mrs. Parks not telling her employer and close co-worker that she had an admirer. Her husband was certain that there was a new man in her life, and he did not seem highly motivated to lie about that. Why not tell the person she worked with every day, given that it was something one would naturally talk about? There had to be a reason for that silence. Undoubtedly, it was that Mr. Kincade told her not to tell Mr. Roeder above all. The notion that the information would set off alarm bells for the latter seems far-fetched, but Mr. Kincade was a man with a guilty conscience."

"You said earlier that if there was a clue in the tarot cards it was in the one called 'The Lovers,'" Lynda reminded him. That's when Mac had outlined his theory that Kincade set up an appointment for a tarot reading earlier that day, asking Quant not to write it down. "Do you think that's what was going on? Was Zoraida Quant trying to identify her killer in the last moments of her life, knowing that Kincade was Dixie Parks's hidden lover? That maybe she laid that card out with her dying breath?"

I'm pretty sure Mac saw that one coming.

"It seems unlikely to me, but we can never know. I will say this, however: One of the other cards on the table when Ms. Quant died was Justice. And I have great confidence that justice will be done in the matter of her murder."

Chapter Twenty-Five
Death of an Alibi

PHOEBE FARLEIGH SIGNED ON as Kincade's defense counsel, but I didn't think she'd have any better success there than she was having with her case for Troy Braggs. And that was a disaster.

BRAGGS ALIBI CHANGES STORY was the headline on Johanna's front-pager, which began:

> Robin Hauser, who told police she was with accused killer Troy Braggs when Braggs's girlfriend Betty Erlanger was shot through the heart on Valentine's Day, now says she was home that evening and will testify so in court.
>
> "I lied to protect a man who was unworthy of my love," she said in an interview after leaving the office of Sussex County prosecutor Marvin Slade.
>
> Hauser has been promised immunity from prosecution on charges of perjury in her sworn statement to police, according to a person familiar with the situation.
>
> Zoraida Quant, who claimed to be an eyewitness to the Erlanger murder and identified

Braggs as the killer, was herself murdered on Tuesday, September 3, the day the Braggs trial began. Carson Kincade, a local investor, has been indicted in connection with her murder and that of her client Dixie Parks, with whom he was having an affair. However, before her death, Quant signed a witness statement which Slade said he plans to enter as evidence.

I was pretty sure that Slade himself was the "person familiar with the situation." Running for re-election, he was eager to see his name in print in a positive context. At this writing, it seems unlikely the prosecutor's office will get a new name on the door.

"Nice piece of luck, Hauser coming forward like that," I told Mac.

"Luck? I sincerely doubt that."

And he was right, of course. It turned out that Gibbons told Hauser about Laurie Meeker visiting Braggs in jail, and even tipped her off when the nurse was likely to pay the bad boy a visit. Result: A three-way shouting match, immediately followed by Hauser visiting the prosecutor. I guess you could say that Braggs's alibi died that day, as did his chance of escaping a long prison sentence.

"Love and money are the most common motives for murder, old boy," Mac pontificated in the Mac Cave one evening not long after. "The intertwined Erlanger, Quant, and Parks murders involved both."

*Turn the page for a bonus novella, **The Puzzle of the Purple Beret**, featuring Lynda Teal Cody and Kathleen Cody McCabe!*

The Puzzle of the Purple Beret

A Kate McCabe & Lynda Cody Mystery

1.

MY ADORABLE HUSBAND, Jeff Cody, insisted that I let my journalistic juices flow in print and write the story of that purple beret business for those of you who won't happen to hear my podcast about it. "You're the reporter," said the man who wrote 15 McCabe & Cody true crime books before this one. Cute.

There's a backstory, of course; there always is. But I only became involved with the tangled romantic relationships of Mona Lisa Carlotti on the day of the crime. The first crime, I mean.

My gal pal Sister Polly Malone, whom Jeff likes to call Triple M (for Mary Margaret Malone), dragged me into her science-fiction book club some years ago as a way for me to have some adult company at least once a month. That assumes, of course, that a group of women calling themselves the Captain Nemo Society are adults.

So it was that on that first Tuesday in October, dinner consumed, I left the three Cody offspring in Jeff's care and headed off to Mo's Mysteries & Marvels bookstore, expecting an evening of enjoyable but not necessarily talk-about-it-the-next-day book chat.

Said chat began before the meeting, almost as soon as Polly got into my car for the ride to the store.

"Did you read the book?" she asked, after telling me how much she loved my turquoise necklace.

"Not all of it," I admitted. "It got to be heavy lifting for me about two-thirds in."

We're always honest with each other, such as the time Polly told me I should marry Jeff instead of joining her religious order. (Being taught in childhood by my Italian grandmother to obey nuns and religious sisters, I did so.)

"The ending sucks," Polly said, using language she usually reserves for our girl talk and (I suspect) perhaps her counseling of individuals incarcerated at the Erin city jail.

"You mean Mac would call it 'suboptimal'?"

"Something like that."

We may have giggled.

Sebastian McCabe is a supposedly silent partner with Mo Russert in the mystery and science-fiction store that carries her name. He doesn't appear in this story in person, although his large shadow hangs over it at times and his name will be evoked on occasion. You have been warned.

MO'S MYSTERIES AND MARVELS, offering both new and used (even a few rare) tomes of mystery, fantasy, science fiction, and horror, occupies the spacious first floor of a former fire station on Water Street. It closes at 6 p.m. every day, but re-opens later twice a month for the meetings of the Captain Nemo Society (first Tuesday), and the Poisoned Pens mystery writing group (fourth Monday). Mac and/or Jeff sometimes honor the latter with their presence.

Polly and I were almost the last to arrive. Sally Fair, Holly Burdette, and Louise LaRosa already had glasses of wine in their hands, and Mo provided ours as soon as we'd finished the hugging ritual. Mo is in her early fifties but looks younger, with a freckled face and dark bangs. It doesn't bother me a bit that Jeff dated her a couple of times some years earlier when our romance was on pause. (How could it bother me? Mo called me first for a rating before accepting Jeff's dinner invitation. Grading on the curve, I gave him four and a half stars. But Mo married Jonathan Hawes, the mortician, in a destination wedding some years after Jeff and I walked down the aisle.[15] We are all friends.)

We chitted and chatted for a while, until our youngest member, chestnut-haired Sally Fair, looked at her Apple Watch and said, "I don't know why my friend Mona Lisa isn't here, but maybe we should start without her."

"Not to gossip," said Louise LaRosa, an apple-shaped woman who works in the county prosecutor's office, "but she was in a big ruckus with her boyfriend at Gatsby's pub on Friday. They were very loud. I couldn't help but hear the word 'gambling.'"

"How hard did you try not to hear?" asked Holly, who is Chief Oscar Hummel's right-hand woman in the Erin Police Department.

"Not very. I was enthralled."

Although I hadn't met Mona Lisa Carlotti, who was to join the group for the first time that night, I knew that she was one of Sally's fellow lawyers, though in a bigger and more buttoned-down firm. Her being late should have been a clue

---

[15] As recorded by Jeff in "A Destination Murder" in *Murderers' Row* (MX Publishing, 2020).

that something was amiss, but apparently my Spidey sense is lacking.

"Well, let's get started," Mo said, taking a seat without spilling her Cabernet Sauvignon. "What did everybody think of the book?"

"I thought the ending was suboptimal," Polly said.

The book in question was *Sunbelt*, written by literary agent Carol Landis from an idea by her murdered ex-husband, James Ivanhoe, an Erin native.[16] His original manuscript was destroyed by his killer, but the outline survived, and Landis brought it to life. The story is set in an alternate timeline in which the Confederate States of America exists as a rogue state in control of crucial metals needed for the lithium-ion batteries used to store the solar energy on which the world depends.

"I agree," Sally told Polly. "The time-travel trope creates a logical inconsistency that just doesn't work."

"Only if you think about it," Louise said.

"Oh, *that* was Sally's mistake," Holly said. "She thought about it."

We bantered on like that for another wine-fueled half hour or so until the door opened (Mo hadn't locked it because this was Erin) and in walked a woman in her early thirties. She had long raven hair in natural curls, a buff body, and brown eyes behind dark-framed glasses for a touch of gravitas. Take away the glasses and she was an Italian beauty like a da Vinci painting, but not the one you're thinking of.

"Sorry I'm late," Mona Lisa Carlotti said.

"Tough day at work?" Sally asked as Mo handed the newcomer a glass.

---

[16] Jeff covered that in *Erin Go Bloody* (MX Publishing, 2016).

"I've just been to the police station to make a report," the latter said. "I was robbed on my way here."

"!!!!!!"

"??????"

That was six voices simultaneously erupting in shock and curiosity. When we'd settled down and Mona Lisa had had more than a sip of wine, she explained.

"I'd just left the condo and was heading for my car when somebody came up behind me and stole my Basque beret right off my head. I was stunned. By the time I looked around all I could see was a fleeing figure in a black balaclava. I couldn't even tell whether it was a man or a woman."

"Good thing they didn't get your purse," Holly said.

"He or she didn't try."

"What did the beret look like?" Polly asked.

"Why?"

"I don't know. That just seems like a question Sherlock Holmes would ask. Or maybe Hercule Poirot."

"It was purple, all-wool, eleven inches in diameter. It wasn't very valuable, certainly not worth attacking me for. I think I paid fifty or sixty dollars for it online."

"This sounds like we're in the middle of one of Edward D. Hoch's Nick Velvet stories," Mo said. She was a mystery fan long before she became a mystery bookstore co-owner.

"I've read some of those," Louise put in. "The gimmick is that Velvet is a thief who only steals things that have no value, and he charges a huge fee for it. Every story has a title that begins 'The Theft of the.' I remember it was a toy mouse in one story and a circus poster in another. The kick is always finding out why the client was willing to pay big for something that seemed worthless. Very clever, I always thought."

"Charming," Sally said, not sounding especially charmed. "But this isn't fiction."

"I hope not," Mona Lisa said with a laugh. "If I were a character in a story, I'd rather be the hero. Anyway, it was probably a prank or a scavenger hunt, something like that. I just thought it was my duty to report it. I'll order a replacement hat and have it by the day after tomorrow. I'm not going to let some jerk spoil our evening. Obviously, you all know who I am. Who are each of you?"

Sally made the introductions, and the book discussion resumed.

2.

THE NEXT MORNING, AS previously arranged, I grabbed a coffee at Beans & Books with Jeff's sister, Kate McCabe. As a novelist and podcaster I set my own hours, and ditto to some degree for Kate as an award-winning illustrator of children's books and adjunct professor of art at St. Benignus University. And since both of us spend a lot of time in our home office or studio, we like to get together sometimes to socialize in another venue (and without our beloved menfolk).

"Mac isn't dealing so well with Rebecca's move to New York," Kate told me, looking up from her café latte. I was deep into my cappuccino and enjoying the coffeehouse atmosphere.

"What does he say about it?"

"Nothing. That's how I know he isn't taking it well. When have you ever known Mac to be silent? Me neither. But these days he just goes galumphing around looking gloomy. He needs a mystery to solve!"

Jeff has never reported (and maybe never noticed) that his sister Kate is a gorgeous woman, with an Irish colleen sort of face, green eyes, and piles of red hair. But at that moment, with her mind on her melancholy mate, she looked stressed.

"Well, I have a mystery," I said, "and I told Jeff about it at breakfast this morning while he was trying to read the paper. But he claims that Mac is involved in what he called a crisis du jour at SBU, something to do with campus politics. He probably just doesn't think my mystery is worthy of those two supersleuths because there's no dead body involved. At least not yet." I hope that last sentence didn't sound too hopeful.

"What's up?" Kate dutifully asked.

Summoning my well-honed reportorial skills, I gave her the scoop on the theft of the purple beret.

"That's not exactly the crime of the century," Kate said.

"Which is exactly what makes it so interesting!"

At that point, my phone pinged with a text from Jeff which said, *"Are you busty?"* That kind of threw me off for a second. I mean, who would know the answer to that question better than Jeff Cody? But then I got it and responded, *"Yes, but I'm not busy."* Jeff came back with, *"Where is autocorrect when you need it?"* We continued back and forth in our usual frisky way until I informed him that I was with his sister. *"Oh. Well, have fun. Tell her hi. Catch you later."*

My warm response to that need not be recorded here. The love of my life is good-looking, supportive, funny, and—weird though he is in some ways—apple-pie normal compared to my parents (who have been what I call "divorced, with benefits" for decades). Ours is the life I always dreamed of, rambunctious kids and all.

"So," Kate said when I set my phone down, possibly with a smile on my face, "if Mac and Jeff did try to figure out what this was all about, how do you think they would go about it?"

"I don't know about them, but I would brainstorm all the possible reasons, no matter how far-fetched."

"Let's do that."

"Okay." I pulled a reporter's notebook out of my purse. It never runs low on battery power. "Mona Lisa said it was probably a prank or a scavenger hunt." I wrote those possibilities down.

"Or, along the same lines, maybe a high school dare," Kate added. "That could happen. But I suppose the idea that somebody needed a hat or just loves the color purple is a little out of the box."

"I said 'no matter how far-fetched.' That's the only rule of brainstorming." After adding Kate's three notions to the list, I said: "Maybe the hat has some hidden value that even Mona Lisa doesn't know about it."

"Possible, I suppose, but it's more likely that somebody did it just to be mean because they don't like the owner of the hat. A lawyer makes enemies."

"Right," I agreed.

So, at this point I had:

Motives

Prank

Scavenger hunt

High school dare

Need for a hat

Love of color purple

Revenge/hatred

"Then, of course, there's the most likely reason of all," Kate said.

"You mean that the thief is what is technically called a whack job?" I asked, just to be clear.

"That would be the technical term, yes."

"But if it's *not* that, if there's some rational reason behind what looks like an act of lunacy and we figure out what it is and then who stole the beret, this little mystery could be the makings of a heck of a podcast."

"For sure." Kate smiled for the first time that morning, which is a beautiful but not too frequent sight. "And we *will* figure it out. We've got this—McCabe & Cody!"

3.

WE DECIDED TO START with the most obvious storylines, the prank-dare-scavenger hunt scenarios, to the degree that we could. After ordering a refill on the coffees, I called Holly at the police department, Louise at the prosecutor's office, and Polly at SBU campus ministry (even, or maybe especially, college students do stupid things) to see if any of them got a whiff of something along those lines. Not surprisingly, they'd all anticipated me by asking around in their particular spheres for any signs of such nonsense. Result: zero, zip, nada, and goose egg.

By this time, Kate and I were sufficiently caffeinated and taking up space that could be occupied by new customers, so we left the coffeehouse.

"There's not much we can do if the thief is somebody who needed a hat, loves the color purple, or is in need of psychiatric care," Kate pointed out.

"Right. So, let's start with the victim."

"We don't really know her."

"No, but Sally Fair does."

SALLY WAS IN HER office at SladeLaw, which is quartered in a former church on Water Street, a block and a half away from Mo's Mysteries & Marvels. We were lucky enough to catch her between appointments. She looked rather lawyerly, I thought, in a cream blouse, chocolate brown slacks, and a fitted jacket the color of espresso beans, all accented with gold from her ears to her wrists nicely setting off her chestnut hair. Fashionable, but not over-the-top for the courtroom.

"Mona Lisa and I jog together," she said, in answer to my innocent question as to how well the two attorneys knew each other. "Don't you just love her name? Her practice at the Bridges firm is strictly civil, meaning wills and trusts for the wealthy and such, and you know I handle minor criminal cases here as well as bread and butter law. But we were cooperating counsel on a case once and just sort of bonded. So, that's how well I know her—casual friends who sweat together. Why do you ask?"

It was a good question. I wished I had a good answer.

"She's a new member of the Captain Nemo Society, and Lynda's worried about her," Kate supplied. "I'm just keeping my sister-in-law company."

That was all true, though not all the truth.

Sally, whom Jeff once described to me as "smooth as silk but hard as nails when defending a client," gave us a look that reminded me of the stink eye I used to get from my pet poodle when I was a kid. The irony in her voice was loud and clear as she said, "That's very nice of you. And how well I know Mona Lisa matters in that regard exactly how?"

"To be honest, we were also intrigued by what happened to her," I fessed up. "I mean, really, who would steal a hat right off of a woman's head?"

Sally leaned back a bit in her very comfortable-looking chair. "So, you're trying to answer that question. Isn't identifying criminals, thereby creating new clients for SladeLaw, your husbands' forte, ladies?"

"They're busy," I said before moving quickly on. "Here's one possibility that just occurred to me: The theft of her beret could have been meant to discombobulate Mona Lisa, to make her feel unsafe, as a sort of psychological ploy to advance some end game that I don't see right now. Can you imagine that happening?"

"Imagination is not my strong suit, strangely enough for a science-fiction fan. Erica"—that's Erica Slade, her boss and southwest Ohio's leading criminal defense attorney— "tells me I need to work on that."

"What Lynda means to ask," Kate interpreted, "is whether Mona Lisa might inspire somebody to attack her for the reasons mentioned? Do you think she's that sort of person?"

Sally ruminated for a while, and then said, "I think anybody might inspire anybody else to do anything, given that the world is full of people who are evil and/or irrational. I see that every day, and not just in my practice. But here's what I know, off the record: Mona Lisa is a good lawyer, very successful in her career because she is smart, self-confident, and determined. Those same qualities have made her personal life a bit of a mess."

"Old boyfriends?" I asked.

"I can't count that high."

"SO CYNICAL FOR ONE so young," Kate said.

"I suspect that lawyering will do that to you."

We were still on the sidewalk, looking across Water Street to the Ohio River and Kentucky beyond it, when I called Mona Lisa at the Bridges law firm and made a date for lunch. Daniel's Apothecary is not exactly high cuisine, but it's next door to my old stomping grounds at the *Erin Observer & News-Ledger* and there is a certain fun to the 1950s décor. There's a jukebox shaped like the back end of a pink and white Chevy, right below the Route 66 clock. And that server Vern, who also dates from the 1950s, is a hoot. But I'll skip most of the dialogue with her.

Mona Lisa was sitting at one of the black and chrome tables, waiting for us beneath a neon Pepsi sign. We all exchanged handshakes, not yet being at the sisterly hug stage. "What's this all about?" she asked immediately after I introduced her to "my sister-in-law and close friend, Kathleen Cody McCabe."

I could say that she seemed distracted and unnerved, but that would probably be projecting, or confirmation bias, or something of the sort. Though she was dressed in a blue business suit, glasses perched on her head, the scent of Birth of Venus perfume wafting my way didn't shout "lawyer" to me. (My supermodel mother, Lucia Schiaparelli, made the fragrance popular when I was in high school. You probably remember that commercial where she stood in the almost-altogether in a big shell in homage to the Botticelli painting of the same name. If you don't, you're probably too young or not male. Jeff prefers my Cleopatra VII fragrance, bless him.)

"I've been thinking about you all morning and just wanted to be sure you're okay," I said. "That was quite an introduction to our little sci-fi club."

Mona Lisa smiled, though not like the famous painting. Call it rueful, I guess.

"I hope I didn't spoil your evening. Maybe I should have skipped it altogether, but I didn't want that bastard, whoever it was who robbed me, to have even the slightest bit of control over me."

"'Whoever it was,'" Kate repeated. "In the cold light of day, do you have any thoughts about that?"

At this point I wanted to pull out my phone and record this for the podcast, but I sensed that would go over like a vegetarian at a cannibal feast. After this was all over, it might be different. She might be willing to re-enact this conversation in the first flush of her gratitude to McCabe & Cody for figuring it all out. (Or so I hoped.)

By way of answer, the lawyer sent her long, dark curls flying with a shake of the head. "I got nothing."

"You're sure the beret didn't have any value beyond what we know—a simple, not very expensive Basque beret?" Kate pressed.

"No. Of course not."

"It seems most likely the thief was somebody who had it in for you," I said casually, tossing it off as if that just occurred to me. "Have you had any altercations recently?"

By this time Mona Lisa was deep into her "Happy Days Ham Hogie," so she took a while before she said, "I suppose everybody in town has heard about my dust-up with my Significant Other at Gatsby's on Friday."

"I didn't," Vern offered, coming up behind me. "Are we OK on drinks?"

We were OK on drinks.

"Louise LaRosa was there," I said, picking up the thread of the conversation after Vern had removed herself again. "So, yes, everybody in town has heard about it by now. Except Vern, apparently."

Mona Lisa sighed. "I've only recently realized that Bryce—his name is Bryce DeLorean—has a bad gambling habit. I mean *bad*. He got sucked into playing online casino games." The betting company she named has billboards all over Ohio and Indiana. "They send him free credits and even gifts. And why not? He's a sheep, and they've got the shears."

"Wait a minute!" I exclaimed. "I read a story about one of those companies just this morning."

It was in Jeff's beloved *Wall Street Journal*. A former Jacksonville Jaguars employee who embezzled more than $22 million from the team sued a betting company for fueling his addiction by giving him more than $1 million in betting credits, gifts, and expense-paid trips. He was asking $250 million in damages. I'm not making that up.

"It's a successful business model for the gambling companies," Mona Lisa said, her voice dripping venom. "At one point, Bryce had a half-million-dollar six-day hot streak going, but that wasn't enough to clear his debts. And then he lost it all again. I mean, it's so bad I'm trying to convince him he needs professional help. Maybe that's why Autumn left him—Autumn Teague. They lived together until they broke up during the summer and I met Bryce on the rebound when I went to buy a car." You might expect her to smile at the memory, but she didn't. "He works at Brett McGee's car dealership complex, and he sold me a Lexus."

This did not seem the time to say, "Nice wheels!" But that's what I was thinking.

"I don't know why I'm telling you all this," she added.

"Because it's good to talk it out," Kate said. "And maybe us not being your close friends makes that easier."

"Anyway, I haven't talked to Bryce since Friday. I don't know if we're through or not. If we are, that should make Gino happy."

"Another beau?" I asked.

"My brother. He never trusted Bryce. But then, he's always negative about my boyfriends."

"I guess you've had a lot of those," Kate said. That's called "leading the witness" on courtroom dramas.

"I've done my part to keep the male population happy, at least for a time." I took that as an affirmative, accompanied by another rueful smile. "At some point up to now they've always decided I'm too directional, or too wrapped up in my work, or some damned thing."

"Always?"

"Well, I did give Otto Mentzel the boot after Bryce charmed his way into my life."

"I know that last name somehow," I said.

"He's a sweet, unexciting man that I met at the courthouse one day. Not at all what you'd expect from a cop." *Officer Mentzel!* I didn't know he had a first name. "No Drama Otto. Compared to Bryce, he seemed dull. I guess I didn't know how good I had it."

"Who would you think most likely to have grabbed a hat off your head—DeLorean or one of his predecessors?" I asked, finally getting to the heart of the matter.

"Neither! None! What are you saying? Why would any of them bother? I mean, what would be the point of minor harassment like that? Especially since most of them gave me the heave-ho and not vice versa."

Good point! Rationally, it made no sense. But then, whoever said men are rational creatures?

Mona Lisa had another question, not so hard to answer even though it was an abrupt change of subject:

"Isn't Polly Malone a nun?"

"Religious sister, technically," I told her. "Nuns live in convents or monasteries, whereas sisters are out in the world. But 'nun' is close enough. She's part of a women's religious order and took a vow of celibacy."

"Maybe she had the right idea."

4.

"BARRING THE NOT-TOO-PROMISING possibility that the purple beret has some value that's not obvious, I think we're stuck with the 'man scorned' theory even though stealing a hat does seem like a penny-ante form of revenge," Kate said.

"And that means we have to talk to Bryce DeLorean, not only the most recent boyfriend but the one with whom she had the argument on Friday. And after him, maybe Officer Mentzel."

But it was too late in the day by then because my three little darlings would be home from school soon, and my fourth little darling a few hours after that. So, we decided to reassemble and resume our sleuthing pursuits the next day, Thursday.

By that time, DeLorean had been attacked.

The news made Friday's *Observer*, three paragraphs with no byline at the bottom of the local page under the headline **MAN ASSAULTED DOWNTOWN**. From that article, I learned that DeLorean was 45. The rest of the story was old news to me by then. I already knew that around 8 p.m. on Wednesday someone came up behind the car salesman on the sidewalk between Gatsby's and his car, apparently tried to strangle him with a scarf, and then ran away, leaving the scarf. Holly Burdette, after seeing the police report, had called me with all that info on Thursday morning because she knew that (1) DeLorean was Mona Lisa's boyfriend of dubious status, (2) Mona Lisa had been robbed the day before the assault on DeLorean, and (3) I was poking into the purple beret theft (as witnessed by my questions to her earlier about the possibility of high school hijinks being behind it).

"A man's scarf or a woman's scarf?" I asked Holly, rather proud of the question.

"Either. I mean, this was a wool stay-warm scarf, not a silk fashion item, so anybody could wear it."

"The plot thickens," Kate said when I called her with the news. "This can't be a coincidence, what happened to Mona Lisa and what happened to her boyfriend."

"Of course it can! The hit-and-run on Mona Lisa and the near strangulation of a man who happened to be her most recent squeeze could be the work of two different people in the unfolding of a random universe." Rather nice phrasing, I thought. "But I wouldn't advise DeLorean to bet on it. We'll see what he has to say."

Before setting out to chat with him at his place of employment, I called Mona Lisa.

"OMG!" was her first response. Her surprise seemed authentic, from what I could tell. "He isn't hurt, is he?"

"My sources tell me"—I love that expression!—"that he didn't need to go to the hospital. He's fine, just shaken up. So, think of what happened to Bryce as a new piece in a jigsaw puzzle, added to what happened to you. Does it help you see the whole puzzle any better?"

"No, not at all. The whole thing seems batshit crazy!"

Well, I couldn't argue with that.

"And now I feel bad about that spat with Bryce and the way I gave him the cold shoulder afterwards, the poor man."

"He's fine," I said again.

BRETT MCGEE AUTOWORKS is a sprawling complex of car dealerships along I-75 selling Toyota, Honda, Nissan, Chevy, Kia, and Mazda brands, and maybe a few more. Kate and I started with Glen Crowley, the sales manager, whom I knew slightly. (Brett steered me to him for a good deal when I bought Jeff a used New Beetle Final Edition to replace his far-from-new New Beetle.) And one of the things that I knew about Crowley is that he talks too much about things he shouldn't talk about at all. Which is a very good thing indeed to be the recipient of if you are a reporter or, in this case, an amateur sleuth.

He was surprised to learn of the attempted strangling of his top salesperson, but not shocked.

"He's a great salesman but has a low boiling point." Crowley himself looks like a character out of *Guys and Dolls*, about 75 pounds overweight and wearing suspenders. The only thing missing is a cigar in his mouth. "A couple of weeks ago he got into a tussle with Victor Wojtowyez, who is also a top performer. I had to break them apart and remind them that they're not in the fifth grade. They didn't exactly kiss and make up, but I think I convinced them to behave so as to remain part of our team."

"Maybe we should talk to Wojtowyez," Kate said.

"Knock yourself out."

When we found him, over in the Honda section, Wojtowyez turned out to be—Lex Luthor! That is, he had that shaved head thing that's kind of popular with men who are partly bald and decide they might as well go all the way. But he was a thirtyish Lex Luthor in a full suit, and I could practically see muscles rippling beneath his coat.

"Hello, ladies."

I'm pretty sure he thought we were a romantic couple but never mind that. I decided to put our metaphorical cards on the metaphorical table.

"We're not here to buy a car," I said. "We're friends of Mona Lisa Carlotti and we're looking into the attack on her lover, Bryce DeLorean." That was pretty blunt, which I was hoping would shock Wojtowyez into saying something helpful.

"Attacked? What do you mean attacked?" His face did gymnastics and his voice got louder as he talked. The salesman was either gobsmacked or a good actor; he could have been either. "I just saw him twenty minutes ago and he looked disgustingly fine to me."

Kate gave him the news in brief.

"I guess I shouldn't be so surprised," Wojtowyez said at the end. "He must have mouthed off to the wrong person. It was bound to happen sooner rather than later."

"We understand that you got into an altercation with him here on the lot," Kate said.

"It wasn't an altercation; it was a fight. I bruised my knuckles on his jaw." He showed them, as if proud. They were healing nicely.

"What happened?" I asked.

"I was standing near him when a certain young woman arrived, and he was rather specific to me about what he'd like to do with said woman."

"That was a rather strong reaction on your part, don't you think?"

"I wasn't raised to talk about women that way," Wojtowyez said. "Besides, the woman in question was my sister, not that it should have mattered. And another besides, I know DeLorean. He went from keeping a woman, that Autumn Teague lady, to (from what I can tell) practically being a gigolo with some lawyer while he throws his money away on gambling."

He seemed rather invested in the topic of Bryce DeLorean. And also well informed.

"What were you doing last night at eight o'clock?" Kate asked.

"I was here, closing a sale."

"MONA LISA BOUGHT a Lexus from DeLorean," I reminded Kate. "How do you think Jeff would respond if I ordered up one of those with all the options?"

"That tightwad? He'd have a heart attack followed by a stroke, or vice versa."

She knows her brother well. Besides, I'm perfectly satisfied with my classic yellow Mustang. But that didn't stop us from approaching DeLorean at the Lexus end of the lot when we had finished yanking Mr. W's chain.

DeLorean saw us coming and walked our way, a car salesman smile in place. With short, mostly gray hair he was good-looking enough, I suppose, if you like the incredibly handsome George Clooney type. I wouldn't have noticed the slight bruise on his jaw if I hadn't been looking for it. He was dressed in business casual, a sport coat over a polo shirt.

"Good morning," was DeLorean's rather pedestrian greeting.

If what follows makes you wonder how DeLorean won the affections of at least two attractive women, bear in mind that he wasn't putting on his charm offensive for us, being neither potential customers nor potential girlfriends. I made that clear when I blurted out:

"We're friends of Mona Lisa."

"Oh." The smile took a hike and the ambient temperature in our shared space on that October day dropped by about 20 degrees.

"She's worried about you," I added.

"Really?" DeLorean seemed skeptical. "Why?"

"She heard about the assault on you last night."

"How the hell—"

"Word gets around," Kate said.

"Much ado about nothing," DeLorean said. "The a-hole didn't hurt me. I only made a police report because I was rattled. And pissed off. I was plenty pissed off."

"Who do you think the a-hole was?"

"Some random lunatic."

"Not a colleague?" I pressed. We hadn't yet checked out Wojtowyez's alibi that he'd been there on the lot last night.

"I get along well with all my associates."

Was DeLorean self-delusional? Or was he wary of bringing up that unpleasantness with Wojtowyez because it involved comments about a woman? I chose door number three: he probably just didn't want to recall losing a fight.

I tried a different approach.

"How tall was the attacker?" I asked. "Was it a man or a woman?" Might as well lay it all out at once.

"How should I know! It happened so fast, and I'd had a few drinks at Gatsby's. Maybe more than a few." So, he was pissed, as well as pissed-off. Words fascinate me. "All I know is, A-Hole was wearing a black ski mask. They tightened the scarf around my neck until I was close to passing out, then ran. By the time I loosened the scarf and turned around they were too far away for me to catch up."

"Probably not a coach potato," Kate asked.

"Mac is ruled out," I agreed.

"Mac?" DeLorean echoed.

"Her husband, Sebastian McCabe. My guy is Jeff Cody. They're—"

"Buttinskies!" DeLorean said with some vigor.

I changed the subject.

"Look, we're just trying to ease our friend's mind about what happened to you." That was stretching the truth a bit. Actually, it was pulling it like taffy. "This certainly seems like whoever did it was motivated by strong feelings. Perhaps a former girlfriend—"

"Get out!"

"If you insist. We want to talk to your former house-guest, Ms. Teague, anyway." I said that to get his reaction; no need to mention that Otto Mentzel was on our suspect list.

The expression on his face strongly suggested that DeLorean was counting to ten. When he got there, he said:

"That won't help you any. If you insist on butting into this, you'd be better off talking to a former customer of mine named Warren Latimer. He was a *very dissatisfied* customer, really got in my face. A looney-tunes like him might do anything."

5.

"I'M SURE YOU GOT the significance of the assailant's black ski mask," Kate said on our way back to my Mustang.

"If it had teeth, it would have bitten me. Mona Lisa's purple beret thief, gender unknown, wore what she called a balaclava. But whenever I see something called that on one of those British crime shows I think of it as a ski mask."

"I don't think there's a difference."

"So, ski masks not being common in southwest Ohio in early October, there's like a ninety-nine percent chance that Mona Lisa Carlotti and Bryce DeLorean were attacked by the same person," I said. "It could be that the goal was to shake up DeLorean, first by showing that his girlfriend was vulnerable (not knowing about their Friday spat) and then by an attack on DeLorean himself that was never intended to be fatal."

"Unless Mona Lisa made up the story about being attacked," Kate said, "which she could have done to take suspicion off of herself in what she expected to be the strangling of her unwanted boyfriend with whom she is very upset."

"Not bad," I mused. "In fact, that sounds like something Mac would say."

"Thank you!"

I bit my lip in thought until I saw the problem with that: "A squabble over DeLorean's gambling jones might be passionate, but it's not the kind of thing that would lead to a carefully thought-out murder attempt including a false report of her beret being stolen. Not in real life, anyway."

If I ever used the word chagrined, I would say that Kate looked chagrined. "Good point," she acknowledged.

"I think we need to track down DeLorean's unhappy customer."

WARREN LATIMER LIVED IN A large development in a Cincinnati suburb about 20 minutes from Brett McGee's Auto-Works. The community was hundreds of acres, including a park space and a lake, and I was reasonably sure the townhouse owner's manual was about 500 pages of dos and don'ts. Kate and I sat on a bench overlooking the lake, as Latimer had instructed us to do in a brief phone call. (DeLorean supplied the number.) We were there about 10 minutes before the dissatisfied customer showed up, but I had a creepy feeling that he was watching us the whole time.

"What's this about? And who are you?" That was his way of saying hi. We hadn't specified our mission in the phone call, only saying that it had to do with his experience at Brett McGee's. He said he would only meet with us out in the open. You know what they say: Just because you're paranoid, that doesn't mean they're not out to get you.

Latimer was an older guy, 70-something, in a flat cap and a down jacket, a walking stick, and a prissy manner. He looked like a good stiff breeze might have blown him away, and I decided to see if I could supply that breeze.

"Bryce DeLorean, with whom you were involved in a dispute over the sale of an automobile, was attacked last night in Erin," I told him. "Somebody almost strangled him with a scarf."

He wasn't blown away.

"Is he alright?"

"Yes."

"Damned shame. Now, back to who you are."

He didn't mean our names; he already had those. "A friend of ours, who is romantically involved with Mr. De-Lorean, was the subject of a theft that we think might have been carried out by the same person who tried to strangle DeLorean. We're trying to help our friend because we know the Erin police aren't that interested." Here comes the part where I softened the truth a bit. "We understand you've spent a bit of time around the Lexus dealership and thought there's a slim chance you might have seen something."

Latimer threw back his head and laughed. "You expect me to believe that? What a crock! You've made my day!"

"You're welcome," Kate said.

"If you think I had anything to do with what you say happened to DeLorean, you've got another think coming. Look at me! I'm an old man. Besides, I have no issue with him anymore. Granted, DeLorean sold me a real lemon, one thing wrong with it after another from the day I drove it off the lot. When you buy a pricy car like that, you expect better. DeLorean was no help at all dealing with the manufacturer. I did my best to get him fired. But that got Brett McGee interested in the situation, and he got me a replacement car. I'm good! No problem! Not that it's any of your business. Any other questions?"

"What were you doing last night around eight o'clock," I asked, seeing nothing to lose.

"I was at a retirement center about three blocks from here, playing my flute at a concert for the residents. It's a regular gig. Ask the management if you don't believe me. Now, would you ladies like some tea?"

6.

WE DECLINED THE TEA, not being sure what the eccentric Mr. Latimer might put in it.

"Next up, Officer Mentzel and Autumn Teague," Kate said, "in whatever order we can access them. Two presumably very different people, with two very different potential motives."

During the pleasant drive back to Erin, distracted a bit by the glory of early fall foliage, we talked about what we had collected other than those names.

"Males are a strange species," I summarized.

"You got that right."

Beyond that, we didn't have much. Despite his undoubted success as a salesman, Bryce DeLorean had provoked the anger of a customer and a sock on the jaw from a colleague. His attractiveness to women was totally lost on me, other than being good-looking, but then he wasn't trying to sell me a car.

"If Wojtowyez wanted to strangle DeLorean, he probably would have made a complete job of it," Kate said. "Latimer, on the other hand, might well have muffed the business."

"But maybe the man with the scarf didn't muff it," I countered. "Maybe he just wanted to give DeLorean a scare. But then there's the matter of alibis."

"Which sound solid."

"And easy to check out, which means it wouldn't make much sense for our suspects to lie."

"Unless of course they didn't expect two women they'd never seen before to check out those alibis." But her sigh showed that Kate didn't really believe that. She was just covering the bases. "We are getting nowhere fast, Lyn."

"Well, there's still the possibility of a connection between the two crimes, that somebody wanted to unnerve Mona Lisa, maybe just shake her up, but also do some real damage to her current boyfriend."

OFFICER OTTO MENTZEL has appeared occasionally in Jeff's McCabe & Cody accounts, but Kate and I didn't know him except by name. He knew our names, too, and our husbands, of course, which is why he agreed to meet with us in the pocket park across from the police station, a safe distance from Oscar.

"You said this was about Mona Lisa and that I shouldn't mention our meeting to the chief," he summarized accurately. "What's up? Is she okay? That stolen hat business was bizarre, and then what happened to DeLorean . . ."

Mentzel stopped talking and shook his head in apparent vexation. It was a good head, on top of a good body. He was tall, blond, blue-eyed, didn't look a day over thirty, and his physique showed no signs of the fondness for donuts that a familiar cliché ascribes to cops. Also, the word "eye-candy" occurred to me.

"Yes, about what happened to DeLorean," I interjected. "What do you know about that?"

"Just that somebody tried to strangle him but wasn't very good at it. L. Jack"—that's Lt. Col. L. Jack Gibbons, Oscar's assistant chief, but you probably already know that—"told me about the police report, just like he did about the stupid hat trick, because he knew I used to be involved with Mona Lisa. I guess you know that, too."

"She's a friend of ours," Kate overstated, which translated to "we probably know more than you want us to know."

But how well did we know Mona Lisa? Not well, I reminded myself before moving on to say:

"It occurred to us that maybe you aren't happy that your girlfriend left you for DeLorean."

Mentzel wasn't a dumb blond, and I try not to be either. So, I could see that he was adding two and two and not getting four. He knew why I was going there with my comment about DeLorean but chose to underplay his response.

"Well, I don't plan to send Bryce a get-well card," he said, "but I'm glad he wasn't seriously hurt. That would be bad for our crime statistics." He smiled to show that he was kidding. It was a nice smile.

"Don't you think the whole thing is rather odd?" Kate said. "I mean, somebody wraps a scarf around the man's neck as if to strangle him but runs away with the job not even half done and leaves the scarf behind."

Mentzel shook his head. "I get what you're saying, but don't get me started on the strange things I've seen in my job. You haven't got enough time."

I said, "I guess there's no point in asking where you were when DeLorean was attacked." Which, of course, was a way of asking.

"I was bowling with Gibbons and Aurelia Banfield in mixed doubles. Banfield fixed me up with a girlfriend of hers from the National Guard. We had a good time, Jenny and I, but no sparks on either side."

On to Autumn Teague.

WE KNEW FROM MONA LISA that DeLorean's former flame was a server at Bobbie McGee's Sports Bar, currently working an early shift. We managed to arrive just after the normal lunch crowd. When Bobbie herself (Brett's long-time wife) dropped by our table to say hi, hiding her brains under a cowboy hat as usual, we asked her to send Autumn Teague our way.

There's no getting around it, the woman was drop-dead beautiful, with wide violet eyes, a round but not-too-round face, a firm chin, and the body of a volleyball player. Her hair was balayaged, short but not-too-short, and she wore silver-colored earrings in the shape of leaves. She smiled easily, as good servers do. We put a stop to that.

"Ms. Teague? We'd like to talk to you about Bryce DeLorean," Kate said without prelude.

"Does he owe you money?"

"No, we're friends of a friend of his," I told her, giving our names. "This will take a little while to explain. Can you give us a few minutes?"

After a moment's thought, she said, "I can talk to you on my break, not while I'm on the job."

She took our drink orders and disappeared. By her break time we were fairly into our meals. Teague took over one of the two empty seats at our table.

"What's this about?" she asked.

"Bryce was attacked last night," Kate said.

"Oh, no! Is he alright?" Her violet eyes went wider.

"He didn't seem too shook up when we talked to him a few hours ago. You asked about owing money. Did he owe money—to gamblers in nice suits and bad manners, for example?"

"Tell me again who you are?" The word "again" was a courtesy since we'd neglected to do that.

We gave her our names.

"Wait!" she said with some energy. "Are you Lynda *Teal* Cody?" I admitted it, mentally making a quick examination of conscience. What had I done now? But it turned out that my name was familiar to her in a good way. "I loved your book *Ink!* Are newspaper people really that crazy?"

"Crazier." This I knew not so much from my time at the *Observer*, although that staff has more than its share of oddballs, but from my internship years. I worked at three larger papers during my years at the communications college of Ohio University. "I had to tone down the insanity to keep it credible. But Kate asked you about Bryce and gamblers. Does he owe some nasty people money?"

Teague shook her head. "Not the way you're thinking. Bryce only gambles online. Hours of it at a time. It's a sickness." She started to wax nostalgic. "It wasn't like that in the beginning. That was here—where we met, I mean. He was a regular customer, though he hasn't come around since we split. After I moved in with him, he asked me to quit so he could have me to himself. I kept the house in order, cooked, and used his credit card a lot."

This is what's known as being a stay-at-home girl-friend (SAHG). It might sound like good work if you can get it, but Jeff pointed out to me one morning over breakfast that it's not a good thing for the girlfriend's long-term financial health. She's not paying into social security, has no guaranteed right to her boyfriend's finances, no inheritance rights, and no right to the guy's Social Security or pension benefits the way a spouse would.

"Is the gambling why you left him?" I was just being nosey, to be honest.

Teague seemed taken aback by the question. "Y-yes," she said after a while. "That was it. I just couldn't take it anymore, so I called it quits. It was hard to do, not having a job. I couldn't just sit around reading novels—no offense, Ms. Cody—and streaming various versions of *CSI* all day anymore. I had to get work."

"And now you're back here," Kate stated the obvious.

"I got lucky for a change. A server named Jade quit and Bobbie re-hired me."

Time to get down to business. "Who do you think might have tried to strangle Bryce?" I asked.

She hesitated. "Well, I heard he had a blow-up with the new girlfriend, Mona Lisa Carlotti, at Gatsby's last week. Believe me, when you've had a breakup, all your 'friends'"— the word dripped sarcasm (and being married to Jeff Cody, I know sarcasm)—"are only too happy to keep you posted on your ex. But I can't believe Mona Lisa would hurt him. From everything I've heard, she's very nice.

"Now, tell me again why you're asking these questions?"

Again with the again!

Kate laid it out for her in brief: "Lynda said Bryce is a friend of a friend of ours, and that's true, more or less. But it's also true that our friend may have been robbed by the same person who roughed up Bryce. And that person needs to be identified and pay for these crimes."

"Damned right they do." A pause. Then, with a catch in her throat, she added, "You know, I still love Bryce."

7.

KATE WAS BUSY TEACHING an art class the next morning, so I puttered around on my next novel. *Ink* and my first novel, *Bluegrass*, were doing well, and I was hoping for a trifecta. Would it be about a military family or the life of a fashion model? I knew both while growing up, but how could I make it believable—the Air Force bases where I was raised by my father, the summers with my mother's family in Italy, and my mother putting in guest appearances in both places after the divorce (during one of which my father sired my sister)? Who would believe all that? The truth is no excuse in fiction. Such were my bleak ponderings that morning when I was rescued by a frantic phone call from Mona Lisa at about 11:30.

"I'm afraid your friend Chief Hummel is going to arrest me!"

"What!?"

"I'm with Sally Fair, who's acting as my counsel. We just got out of a grilling at the police station. Hair with my DNA was in the scarf wrapped around Bryce's neck. I have no idea how it got there. I didn't attack Bryce!"

"This calls for caffeine. Meet me at Beans & Books, ASAP."

I quickly texted the same to Kate, knowing that she would be free by noon. What I didn't do was try to loop Mac and Jeff in on what was, after all, our case and not theirs. I'd been, let us say, less than fully communicative with Jeff about our sleuthing the day before, and this was no time to catch him up. (I'd managed to distract him from inquiries about my activities by drawing his attention elsewhere. The kiddoes were down for the night, and we were alone at the time.)

Mona Lisa and Sally were both working their phones, parallel playing, when I arrived at the coffeehouse. They kept at it while I ordered my pick-me-up from the counter. Kate was only five minutes behind me.

"So, what happened?" I asked the two lawyers when my sister-in-law and I were settled in.

"Like I said, there was hair in the scarf, and the police sent it to the BCI." That was Mona Lisa.

"Ohio Bureau of Criminal Investigation," Sally interpreted, although I knew that. "They do lab work around the clock for every police department in the state."

"And they said the hair had my DNA, meaning it was my hair," Mona Lisa babbled. "Hummel thinks I tried to strangle Bryce. But I didn't!"

"How did the hair get there?" Kate asked.

A quick shake of the head from Mona Lisa. "I have zero idea."

"You mean, of course, how did *her* hair get there," Sally told Kate. "As a general matter, hair turns up all over the place during police investigations. And especially on clothing. I bet every scarf you own has hair on it."

"Why was your DNA on file?" Kate asked Mona Lisa.

"I'm in a database for genealogical research."

"So Chief Hummel called Mona Lisa in for what he miscalled a 'friendly chat,'" Sally said, using air quotes. "Fortunately, Mona Lisa then called me. The Chief figures that just because she had that public dust-up with DeLorean on Friday, it makes perfect sense she would try to strangle him on Wednesday."

"If I'd tried, I would have succeeded," Mona Lisa put in.

"Probably best to keep that to yourself," I advised.

"Hummel made a big deal about how strong and fit she looks, and how she easily could have been Bryce's would-be strangler, and that there's no proof of the beret theft. He said the theft could have been 'a fairy tale,' in his words, designed to confuse the issue and make Mona Lisa look innocent."

I'd heard this theory before, from Kate, but now there was DNA evidence to back it up.

"Were a big, bearded guy and a handsome redhead part of this 'friendly chat'?" I asked. Air quotes again.

"You mean Sebastian McCabe and your husband?" Sally asked. "We would have mentioned that."

"And Jeff would have told me, eventually, but maybe not until later. Anyway, Oscar must be pretty confident that he doesn't need any help on this one."

"But he does!" Mona Lisa burst out. "Obviously!"

"Did he say anything about arresting you?" Kate asked.

"He didn't have to. He just told me not to leave town, like a cop in a bad movie. Can you get Mac on the case?"

"Not necessary," I said. "We've got this—the other McCabe & Cody team! Is there somebody who might want to help you by hurting Bryce, maybe just as a warning to treat you better, make him fear for his life without really trying to kill him? In other words, who loves you that much?"

"My brother, I suppose. But he wouldn't do that!"

I didn't know much about DNA (and still don't), but I was pretty sure the DNA of a brother and a sister were close, maybe close enough to be confused.

8.

IT WAS SUCH A GOOD theory I didn't want to let it go. Not even after we met Gino Carlotti. I expected Tony Soprano, and I got . . . a former monk (really!) who now works at Winter's Ice Cream about a half-hour from downtown Erin. I don't know what he does, but he has a desk and a nameplate.

"Almost strangled?" he repeated. "That's awful. What a world!"

I would accuse him of quoting the wicked witch in *The Wizard of Oz* if I didn't say that so often myself.

Mona Lisa's older brother was drool-worthy, like my Italian uncles, and about the same age as DeLorean (mid-forties) but with less gray in his hair.

Kate gave him the line we'd decided on during the drive there, which had the advantage of being all true:

"As we told the receptionist, we're friends of Mona Lisa. We're really afraid that the police might charge her with the assault on DeLorean. So, we're wondering whether you have any idea who might have done it?"

He appeared gratifyingly horrified at the word "arrest." Our hope was that this threat to his sister might motivate him to say something useful. A confession would be nice!

"That's . . . that's insane! Mona would never do anything like that. She was robbed herself, just a few days ago."

"We're sure she wouldn't," I assured him. "But somebody did, and it may have been somebody who wasn't happy that DeLorean and your sister were on the outs. Any idea who that might be?" (Yourself, maybe?)

"Personally, I didn't like it when they were on the ins, if that's a word," Carlotti said. "I didn't trust DeLorean. My sister wouldn't tell you this because she feels like a fool, but she lent that jerk substantial sums of money to pay off gambling debts, always on his promise that he would lay off the betting." He took a breath. "I'm sorry, I know gambling is a psychological problem and I should be sympathetic to a man who's hooked. But I find that hard, knowing what he put Mona through.

"There's a Flannery O'Connor story called 'A Good Man Is Hard to Find.' That could be the theme of my sister's life. She's never been able to find a good man, and Lord knows she's tried dozens of them."

Kate's turn: "Just for the record, did you happen to put on a ski mask on Wednesday night, follow DeLorean out of Gatsby's, and wrap a scarf tightly around his neck either in revenge or to warn him off?"

"What! You're crazy! Both of you!"

"That's not an answer." Kate does bad cop better than I do. Good to know.

"I was at volleyball practice with my daughter's high school team," Carlotti said. "I'm the coach. All the team members were there and a lot of their parents."

But he didn't say no.

"MAYBE HE BILOCATED," I told Kate in Winter's parking lot. "Padre Pio could do that. Wasn't he a monk?"

"Yes, but Gino left the monastery—what did Mona Lisa say?—twenty-some years ago. I don't think Oscar or anybody else would buy the idea that bilocation undercuts his alibi. What did we learn from this interview?"

"Obviously, Gino's very protective of his sister, which makes him a good suspect except that he was with a bunch of teenage girls," I said. Remembering myself as a teenager, I shivered at the prospect. Then I remembered I would be living with a teenage girl in just five years. Then I remembered that I was supposed to be thinking about the case. Or rather, two cases. "Gino mentioned the theft of Mona Lisa's beret. We need to get back to the big question: If we don't buy the idea that Mona Lisa made that up to make herself look like a victim, knowing that she was going to attack DeLorean, then what's the connection between that goofy theft and what happened to DeLorean?"

"If there is one," Kate said. "After all, they're really quite different—a nonviolent theft and an assault."

"Still . . . the purple beret is where we came in. It's what we were looking at before somebody gave DeLorean a new scarf. What did we overlook?"

"Nothing! We looked at the idea of a prank, a scavenger hunt, a high school dare, somebody who needed a hat, somebody who loves the color purple, somebody who hated Mona Lisa, and, most convincingly, some nutter."

And then, I had a flash. Call it inspiration, like when I'm plotting a novel, and ideas just pop in uninvited. "Wait a minute! There's one more possibility we never seriously considered. The other day, you said something like 'barring the not-too-promising possibility that the purple beret has some value that's not obvious . . .' Maybe that's it! The Edward D. Hoch trope of the almost worthless item that's worth stealing."

"How could it have a value that's not obvious, Lyn?"

"As a hat, it couldn't, given the fact that Mona Lisa bought it and told us what she paid for it. But maybe there was something *in* the hat that was valuable to the thief."

"Like what?"

"Like a few strands of Mona Lisa's hair, which would be quite likely to make its way into the beret. Think CSI, like the thief did."

"Oh!" Kate got it. "And if you're right, that tells us who the thief is, doesn't it? And the connection to the De-Lorean strangling attempt."

9.

"YOU AGAIN!" BRYCE DELOREAN, standing in the doorway, looked at Kate and me as if he were smelling something unpleasant and we were it. It was evening, the Cody kids were in bed, and we'd tracked DeLorean down at his home, a showy place probably loaded down with mortgages. I may have given Jeff the impression that Kate and I were having a girls' night out. Which we were, I guess.

"I hope you're here to apologize for wasting my time," DeLorean went on. "From what I hear, the cops have just about proved it was Mona Lisa who laid into me. So much for amateurs!"

"You heard wrong," I told him. "But now you're going to hear right. This won't take long unless you make it take long. I'll start by telling you what we had wrong from the start of this business, because the truth puts a different light on everything. We thought that Autumn is the one who ended your relationship. That's what Mona Lisa believed and what she told us, but it's not true, is it?"

"I don't see how that—"

"Because of your gambling, you no longer had the money to support her in the manner to which you accustomed her," Kate said. We were double-teaming him. "A more honorable man would have leveled with her and suggested that she get a job, but you gave her the boot. And when others, including us, assumed that she was the one who ended the relationship, you were happy to let them think so rather than know the truth. And so was she."

Back to me: "When I said something about her leaving you, she looked startled at first but then leaned into it—because if she left you, instead of vice versa, that would mean she had no motive to do the things she did."

"What things? What the hell are you talking about?"

We were going to have to draw this guy a map, verbally speaking.

"Autumn stole Mona Lisa's purple Basque beret so she could get a few hairs to plant in the scarf that she knew she was going to wrap around your neck," I said. "What happened then was just what she wanted and expected to happen—Erin police sent those hairs to the state crime lab, which traced them to Mona Lisa through the DNA."

"Why the hell would she even think of something like that?"

I'd asked myself the same thing, and given myself the answer I gave DeLorean:

"When we talked to her at Bobbie's, Autumn made a reference to watching the *CSI* TV franchise, which constantly uses DNA in its storylines."

DeLorean looked dazed, but Kate piled more on:

"Autumn is a strong, fit woman, just like Mona Lisa, and quite capable of catching you unawares and nearly strangling you."

"Thinking back," I said, "I should have realized that in our conversation with her she showed a remarkable lack of interest in exactly how you were attacked. And when I used the word 'strangled,' she didn't respond with surprise and shock, as you would expect an ex-girlfriend to react if she didn't already know what happened. Another thing about that little chat: She referred to your very public set-to at Gatsby's, which means she knew Mona Lisa would be a suspect in what happened to you."

"Bottom line," Kate said, making sure DeLorean could read the map, "is that you hurt Autumn Teague and she wanted to hurt you back, while at the same time framing the woman who, as my husband might say, displaced her in your affections."

It wasn't hours before he spoke again, it just felt like it.

"Tell Autumn I won't press charges," he said at last, a chastened and perhaps wiser man. "And I'll ask Mona Lisa not to, if she'll talk to me."

"YOU CAN'T PROVE IT," Teague said when we'd laid it all out for her a half-hour later at Bobbie's. We didn't bother to take seats this time.

"We don't have to prove it, since Bryce is being nicer than you deserve," Kate said. "We just wanted you to know that we know. Tomorrow we'll talk to Chief Hummel and tell him what happened. He'll probably believe us. But even if he doesn't, Mona Lisa is safe from prosecution because Bryce knows the truth. And we'll do our best to clear her reputation in the court of public opinion. That means a lot in a town like this, especially to an attorney."

"It would be nice if you sent her the beret back, by the way," I added. "You could put it in the mail with no return address."

After a moment's thought, Teague said, "You're not as smart as you think you are, you two. You said I was out to get revenge on Bryce. Revenge and hurting him had nothing to do with it. I wanted him back. And I thought that would happen if he believed Mona Lisa was crazy and tried to strangle him. I wasn't lying when I said I still love him."

"AUTUMN CAN HAVE HIM," Mona Lisa assured me when I ran into her on Main Street a few days later. She was coming out of Beans & Books with Otto Mentzel, and they were holding hands.

A Few Words of Thanks

Jeff Cody and I get our names on the covers, but these books always owe a lot to our collaborators in Team Cody. So, let's round up the usual suspects. My thanks to:

Ann Brauer Andriacco, for providing much of the plot for *The Puzzle of the Purple Beret* during a vacation in Barbados, and for so much more;

Jeff Suess, for being the first reader of the book;

Steve Winter, yet again, for giving the manuscript the benefit of his engineering eye and for making many suggestions that went beyond copy editing;

Peg Hausman, a long-time friend and short-time team member, for being the final copyeditor (although she, too, went far beyond the call of duty).

Any errors that remain are mine, not theirs.

Publisher Steve Emecz remains a pleasure to deal with. MX Publishing is a social enterprise venture that is both enterprising and venturesome.

About the Author

Dan Andriacco has been reading mysteries since he discovered Sherlock Holmes at the age of about nine and writing them almost as long. His first published work, however, was a Sherlock Holmes pastiche short story in 1990. The McCabe-Cody series began in 2011.

After almost 24 years as a reporter and business editor of a daily newspaper, Dan served as communications director for a religious nonprofit for 20 years. He holds a master's degree in religion and a doctorate in ministry.

A Baker Street Irregular ("St. Saviour's, Near King's Cross"), Dan is editor of the BAKER STREET JOURNAL, Most Scandalous Member (leader) of the Tankerville Club of Cincinnati, and a member of numerous other scion societies of the BSI. He also wears bow ties. You can follow his long-running blog at www.danandriacco.com and his Facebook Fan Page, Dan Andriacco Mysteries.

Dan and his partner in criminous endeavors, Ann Brauer Andriacco, have three grown children and six grandchildren. They live in Cincinnati, Ohio, USA, about 40 miles downriver from the town Erin, which is located on no map.

Also from MX Publishing

Visit www.mxpublishing.com for dozens of other Sherlock Holmes novels, novellas, short story collections, Conan Doyle biographies, Holmes travel books, and more.

MX Publishing is the award-winning, world's largest independent Sherlock Holmes Book publishers with over 150 new authors and 500 new Sherlock Holmes stories in print.

On Facebook:
https://www.facebook.com/BooksSherlockHolmes/

On X:
https://x.com/mxpublishing

On Instagram:
https://www.instagram.com/mxpublishing/